North Kill

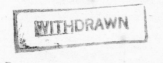

JAMES WOOD

North Kill

Hutchinson of London

HUTCHINSON & CO (*Publishers*) LTD
3 Fitzroy Square, London W1

London Melbourne Sydney Auckland
Wellington Johannesburg Cape Town
and agencies throughout the world

Set in Intertype Pilgrim
Printed in Great Britain by The Anchor Press Ltd
and bound by Wm Brendon & Son Ltd
both of Tiptree, Essex

ISBN 0 09 122010 6

Just a wee story
for
Hilary and Mo

I

Detective-Constable Dick Rimmer stood at the foot of the table and watched the surgeon's hands working with the bistoury. The light overhead glinted back in sharp reflection from the stainless steel haft, but the searching blade had dulled with the initial work of the incision though its edge remained razor keen and steady in the gloved hands as it cut into the cervical muscular tissue immediately below the patient's left ear. The knife hardly interested him: his mind was in other directions, on other planes. But this was one way of officially dodging the column if only for a few minutes. He had a right to be here – in a way.

He hardly heard the surgeon's mild grunt.

The surgeon said: 'Fine specimen of a man,' and drove the tip of the knife deeper, cutting upwards, gently but firmly, knowing exactly where the blade had to go. 'Fine specimen, all right.'

'It's the long holiday, Doc,' Rimmer said sourly. 'Does them the world of good, up yonder in the fine fresh air, and that.'

'How long?' The surgeon withdrew the knife and his fingers searched a kidney tray for a forceps.

'Five years. Lucky to get away with that, too.'

'You here then – when he was . . .'

'I was in Central Division then, Doc.'

'With Frank Wishart?'

'My sergeant – Frank,' Rimmer said, and found a pack of cigarettes, thinking about Frank Wishart being a superintendent and himself still a plodder.

'When'd you transfer to North Division?' the surgeon asked, poking into the gaping cavity with the forceps.

7

'Five – nearly six years back.' Rimmer craned closer to the locus of surgery expectantly. 'Any luck?'

'Have to get a bit farther in.' The gloved hand picked up the knife again, held it up to the light while spectacled eyes peered at the tip before it was discarded for another. 'Ever tried operating with a dessert spoon?'

'Never tried – operating – full stop, Doc. Better you'n me.'

'It's all right. Never quite get the same job twice. Not exactly the same. Makes it interesting, as the old dears would say.'

'Aha. Fag, Doc?'

'In a minute. Think I'm on to one now.'

Rimmer placed a cigarette on the edge of the table, level with the patient's knees, and the surgeon glanced at it, nodded thanks and went back in with the forceps. Jock Cameron was a large man, and the hands inside the rubber gloves were massive and covered along their backs with ruddy hair and large freckles. They had placed numerous tries on the Rugby field, extracted suppurating appendices, administered anaesthetics, tied off countless bleeding points, delivered babies, dealt bridge hands with frightening speed, and amputated any of the human limbs you cared to mention. But they were tidy hands. Jock Cameron disapproved of making a bloody mess literally. Made cleaning up all the more irritating.

The right hand slowly withdrew the forceps and dropped a small metallic particle into a kidney dish. Rimmer heard the clank it made in the dish as he lit his cigarette and blew smoke into the beam from the overhead light.

'One,' he said quietly, 'two to come.'

'I'll get one of them from the other side. Can feel it under the skin. No problem there, Dick.'

'Must've been real close – going right through, Doc.'

'Fairly close. Not close enough to burn, though.'

'They had to go through the car window first,' Rimmer said.

'That'd explain it. Now for the next wee chap.' The knife made a second incision and went deeper.

There was an indefinable odour of bitterness in the air. It wasn't the cleaning spirit – it was . . . just bitterness, and chill. The sour-faced detective-constable in the charcoal grey lounge suit, white shirt and ultramarine blue tie tipped his hat back from his brow and sniffed the bitterness, and blew more smoke into the beam of the light. His ears caught the sound of brittle crunching somewhere inside the patient's neck. Jock Cameron grunted again and looked for a longer knife.

Rimmer said: 'Aye,' and nodded.

'Hmm?'

'That one's not going to be much good – when you got it.'

'It'll be fragmented a bit, I'd say. And pretty flat.'

'All right if I have a look?'

'Help yourself, sure.'

Rimmer moved to the surgeon's side and picked up a piece of tissue paper and pinched it about the first extraction in the kidney bowl. Holding it up to the light, he squinted at it and said: 'Could be a three-two.'

'Bit smaller, I thought,' Cameron offered as he cut farther into the patient's neck.

'Two-five, then. Jacketed, too.' Rimmer dropped the bullet back into the tray and went back to the foot of the table.

'I'd reckon on it being a two-five, yes.' Cameron straightened himself, picked up the cigarette and lit it with a book match, stretching himself as he inhaled. 'Small calibre penetrates better.'

'But doesn't pack the punch.'

'Can't have it all ways, Dick. Why'd they do it?'

'Tell you when I find out.'

'Aye. Any ideas who it could have been?'

'One or two – four, in fact. He isn't the friendly type.'

'No, I suppose not. What'll he get – if you do find . . .'

'Were it up to me, I'd give him three hearty cheers and buy

9

him a half gill and a pint. Usual – life – ten at the most. Piece of bloody nonsense.'

'But you'd give him three hearty cheers. Great.'

'Saves us a bit of work, that's all. The more they cut themselves up, the better I like it. Common sense, Doc. Common sense.'

Cameron yawned and picked up the forceps for another try.

Rimmer caught the infection and stifled his own yawn. He was happier than he had been for some time. Not that this applied to his duty at all: it applied to his domestic life. His wife, who had disappeared with a haberdashery salesman and had been living with him for three years and two months down in Lossingley, hadn't chosen to return within the stipulated period of three years, and now he had filed a desertion suit and had provided more than enough evidence of same, and adultery, to satisfy a dozen Lord Justices.

Not only that, but he'd changed all the locks in the flat, given her effects to a suitable charity, and had installed a half-caste young woman as a part-time housekeeper. He felt, and quite reasonably as any reasonable individual would agree, that a mild adultery session on his own part would not be entirely out of place . . . in view of all that had come to pass. A prolonged and painstaking study of human nature in all its frailties was by now convincing him that a modicum of applied tenderness and attention would steer Cherry Landry, if not directly into his long-neglected double bed, then across the settee in the small lounge.

Thinking thus pleasantly he neglected to remain with the present and consequently realized that the dog-end of his cigarette was slowly burning its way through his lower lip. Rimmer half-turned his head and spat the offending dog-end into a trash bin on the floor.

'You going to have a duffy inside, Doc?' he asked, in an effort towards reorientation, which was necessary if regrettable.

'Not unless the P.F. hands me down an order for same.'

'Hmm.'

'Why d'you ask?'

'Just asking.'

Cameron examined him through the spectacles. 'You look as if a decent three-course dinner wouldn't kill you immediately.'

'I was thinking more of a three-course something else, Doc.'

'Oh. I might have guessed.' The surgeon knew all about the many and varied departmental personal problems. 'Well, good luck.'

'Thanks.' Rimmer smiled and feathered his fingers along the naked soles of the patient's feet. 'I'm what you'd say at a – a . . . a fine turning point in time, Doc.'

'I'm buggered if I can sense what's behind . . .'

'When does adultery become fornication, Doc – or vice versa?'

Cameron absently tapped the heavy curve of his jaw with the tips of the stained forceps, his eyes half-closing against the smoke of his cigarette. 'You know, that's a good question.'

'The job, Doc – asking good questions,' Rimmer said.

'Glad I'm an honest quack,' Cameron said thankfully, and probed for the malformed slug with the forceps. 'I'd say – I'd say that in your present circumstances, it would be known as a borderline case.'

'Borderline. Hmm.'

'Just the same. Dick, I'd keep off the nest until . . .'

'I know how to be careful, Doc.'

'Never know these days. Here it is. Nasty one.'

The bullet, upon striking home, had shed part of its metal jacket, had torn down one side and had the general appearance of a mushroom that had been half-trodden on. Wisps of human tissue adhered to the ragged edges of the jacket. It was dropped beside the first one in the kidney tray. Then Cameron swiftly nicked the other side of the patient's neck, pressed gloved fingers on each side of the neat incision, pressed more firmly, and the third projectile popped out and rolled on to the floor with a dull thud on the polished linoleum. Rimmer fielded it with another piece of tissue and placed it in the kidney tray.

'Looking inside?' he inquired.

'No need for that this time.' Cameron removed his gloves, tapped the ash of his cigarette and took one last suck at the dog-end before tossing it into the sink where he went to scrub down. 'For his age,' he said, 'he's one of the finest specimens I can remember seeing. Seems to me a pity it had to happen as it did. He might have lived to be a hundred.'

'I'm crying my eyes out,' Rimmer answered sourly, staring down at the pateint's naked feet.

The patient on the table was Anthony Bolesco, fifty-six, white, a British national of Italian extraction, height six foot two, dark complexion, eyes blue, weight one hundred and ninety-two pounds, scars of gunshot wounds on left shoulder and hip. So much for physical identification. Official identification ran: Criminal Records Office Number 467/822/94.* Convicted on charges of extortion, fraud, intimidation of Crown witnesses, and robbery with violence. The latter of which had earned him the ridiculously light sentence of only eight years' detention, five of which he had served until some crackpot parole board had foolishly decided to turn him loose on long-suffering society once more. And there had always been the hope that he'd lead the way back to wherever it was he had planted the considerable sum of money before being apprehended, Rimmer reminded himself ruefully, for there would be no hope of recovering the loot now.

Anthony Bolesco, one-time boss of the North Side mobs, had been released from Carronhead Prison at seven-thirty that same morning.

Rimmer checked the time on his wrist-watch against the clock on the wall beyond the operating table.

An orderly joined them and went to speak to Doc Cameron

* This is no kind of C.R.O. number sequence.

at the sink. The man spoke in a mere whisper and the surgeon was nodding and reaching for a towel while the man untied his *smock's* tapes behind his back and removed the garment.

Rimmer squared up his hat, tightened his necktie and arranged the peaks of his shirt collar. He picked up the kidney tray and its contents.

Anthony Bolesco – precisely four hours and twenty minutes had passed since his execution.

Not murder – execution. It was so obvious.

And a classic of its kind.

The detective-constable whistled the opening bars of *Hey, Johnny Cope* as he left the bitter-chill precincts of the place and made his way across to North Division.

The execution had been a real classic.

Solving it would probably fall right into his reluctant lap, too.

Reflecting upon that, Rimmer ceased to whistle.

A faint trace of snow hugged the pavement edges as he walked up the street to headquarters.

2

The execution was the last thing any of them expected to happen.

At seven-fifteen that morning Tony Bolesco was marched into the deputy-governor's office at Carronhead Prison by the chief officer. He stood smartly to attention for five minutes while the D.G. delivered his usual well-chosen verbal tirade, read the riot act, and eventually offered his right hand across the desk. Bolesco shook it warmly and took a smart pace to the rear and, upon getting the word from the chief beside him, made a smart right turn and marched out.

In the reception yard the day shift were coming on duty, lined up for sticks and whistles inspection. Bolesco ignored them. He waited for the chief to unlock the wicket gate and passed through it with a word of farewell to his escort. The wicket was relocked behind him.

A bronze Chrysler Avenger's engine was revved gently. Bolesco nodded to the driver, but he spent a few seconds looking at the vastness of the sweep of the grey sky before getting into the car.

'Hospital first, Tony?' the driver asked him.

'Give it a minute, Chick. Promised a boy I'd give him a lift into town.' Bolesco's eyes looked out across the open countryside, getting used once more to the colours, dull though they were on that bleak morning. He didn't say anything while they waited for the other released man to appear through the wicket gate.

When Lynch did appear, Bolesco reached behind him and swung one of the rear doors open for him. Lynch trotted across the few yards from the gate and got into the car.

'Right, Chick, take it away. We drop Pat here at the first bus-stop in town and then you know where.'

'Hi, Pat. How's the boy?' the driver said.

'Better when I get back in the groove.' Lynch laughed when they laughed. They all knew the sort of groove he meant.

Bolesco had his own groove already organized. She was well-named; Joy. And she worked as manageress in one of his partially owned entertainment enterprises, the Crystal Club on Chesterton Drive. But Joy, and he, would have to wait for it. He had to see his father first.

Lynch said: 'I'll come round in the morning then, Tony.'

'About eleven.'

'And bring . . .'

'Come alone. I told you that before.'

'Sure, so you did. Eleven – that's all right with me.'

The driver kept half an eye on the rear mirror. The traffic behind consisted of a mobile shop, a green truck, a kid on a motorcycle, and a mini. Chick kept the speedometer needle just touching fifty. Tony had a thing about fast, erratic driving. The mini was space-jinking up towards them; presently it pulled out and overtook the Avenger.

'All you want me to take is a change of gear?' Lynch asked from the rear seat.

'That's all. I'll fix up whatever else you'll want. But be prepared to stay out of circulation for at least a week. And! No chat about what's on!'

'Sure. No chat, Tony. I'm not altogether an . . .'

'Just remember that. No chat!'

'A week – out of circulation,' Lynch said. 'That's going to mean a hell of a lot of groove before ten o'clock in the morning.'

'Make the most of it,' Bolesco told him. 'But try not to shag yourself silly, that's all. It's going to be a fast one.'

'Make it as fast as you like,' Lynch said. 'I'm all for it.'

Behind them, the mobile shop had turned off the main highway. In its place was the green truck and the kid on the motor-cycle immediately behind that. He was still fifty yards behind them when the car entered the built-up area. Then the kid took a left-hander and disappeared from view. The morning commuter traffic enclosed them until they found a bus-stop and dropped Lynch.

'See you, lads,' Lynch said, waving them on.

'See you, Pat,' Chick nodded and wound up his window.

Bolesco asked the driver: 'How was the old man when you saw him last – when was that?'

'Monday night. You'll get a hell of a shock. Hardly anything left – of him.'

'I'm used to shocks. They die that way in yonder, too, you know.'

'Different when it's your old man, though.'

'Yeh.'

The matter of his father's terminal illness had also come under the consideration of the parole board. They had gone as far as to discover the relationship that existed between father and son. It was common knowledge that Anthony Bolesco, despite his past record, worshipped both his parents. His mother had passed on four years earlier. The prison padre's accurate report of the prisoner's moral breakdown at the time had also been recorded for the board. The board had been moved by the fact that a mature man who had survived some of the most bitter engagements of the jungle war against the Japanese could be so stricken. And his record of and decoration for distinguished conduct had not been over-looked.

The Avenger drew up in the hospital car park at nine-ten.

'Want me to come in?' Chick asked.

Bolesco shook his head.

The driver produced a brandy flask from a door pocket.

Bolesco shook his head again.

'Think you'd better, Tony. Go on.'

'Go in there stinking?'

'They understand about all that. Happens all the time. Go on.'

Bolesco drank some of the brandy and waited for several minutes until he could feel the partially relaxing effects of the spirit. Then he went into the hospital. A fawn-coated porter escorted him to the ward and said he'd come back later and wait for any instructions. While Bolesco was in the ward with his dying parent, the porter made a formal telephone report to Duty-Sergeant Steve Pearson at North Division, giving the mobster's time of arrival, full details of the vehicle that awaited him outside, the description of the driver, and asked for further orders. Steve Pearson told him to ensure the adjacent presence of a Blue Ford Escort somewhere on the forecourt and, it being there, to wait until Bolesco had left the premises and then to return to the office. The porter nodded at the telephone, and hung up.

A minute later he was in the ward, carrying a napkin-covered tray of cups and saucers. A young nurse had already brought in the tea, and they proceeded to serve the four aged male patients.

The porter asked the tall visitor: 'Would you care for tea, sir?'

Bolesco began to shake his head, and then he said: 'Yes, I think I'd like a cup, thanks.'

'Sugar, sir?'

'Thanks, yes.' Bolesco was holding his father's hand. In his free hand was a crumpled handkerchief.

The old man in the bed lay flat, his eyes half-closed against his pain. The young nurse with a feeding cup spoke to him gently, but he gave no sign that he heard her words.

'Dad,' Bolesco whispered to him. 'The nurse asked if you ...'

'Later, Anthony,' the old man answered with difficulty.

'Maybe I ought to go ... now?' Bolesco said to the girl.

'Best if you stayed a little longer, sir.' She smiled down at him and went to attend to the other patients.

'What can I get for him?' Bolesco asked the porter.

'He has everything he requires, sir. Perhaps if you asked Sister as you go out. Her office is on the left, the second door along.'

'Yeh. Thanks. Look, get yourself some cigarettes.' Bolesco gave the porter a currency note, one of several supplied by Chick in the car.

'We're not permitted to accept...'

'Go on. This is my old man.' Bolesco pushed the note into a pocket of the porter's fawn overall coat.

'Very well, sir. I'll be in the annexe – just ring.'

'Yeh. I understand.'

The porter left the ward and later put the currency note into a box in the Sister's office, after which he devoted himself to a newspaper in the annexe until the visitor chose to ring the ward bell.

Bolesco rang the bell at nine-fifty and was escorted to the front entrance. The porter waited for him to get into the Avenger, raised a hand as the car swept out of the forecourt, and watched the Ford Escort follow. The driver of the Ford was Detective-Sergeant Hugh 'Dusty' Miller and the attractive girl beside him was Policewoman Sheila 'Slim' Summerville, both of them from the branch commonly known as the Untouchables.

The porter took a bus back to North Division and wrote out his formal report.

The Bolesco home was on Elleston Road, a one-way thoroughfare, the house standing on the left of the road as one proceeded north, three feus beyond the intersection with Cartland Avenue.

A recent violent explosion in the city, resulting in major property destruction and multiple injuries and deaths, had given the Gas Board cause to overhaul their pipelines, one of which ran the length of Elleston Road. A team of engineers and workmen were working with a compressor and pneumatic drills on the roadway near the intersection. Three private saloon cars were casually parked on the left side of the road as the Avenger approached the intersection. Behind it was a delivery van, then a break-down truck, and then the Ford Escort, all dropping speed for the halt sign ahead. The air was filled with shattering sound from the drillers on the other kerb.

As the bronze car was about to come abreast of the last of the three parked cars, the driver, apparently unaware of the oncoming traffic behind, half opened his door, causing Chick Harmon to curse and apply his brakes. He was checking in his rear mirror automatically and did not see the erring driver of the parked car. Nor did he hear the rapid volley of small-calibre shots for the sound of the drillers. A shower of small ice-like particles seemed to erupt from beyond Tony. Tony was suddenly leaning his weight against Chick. And a blinding curtain of red colour followed the sickening impact against the driver's forehead.

Chick Harmon awoke just under an hour later in a casualty ward, his head bandaged and with a splitting ache that seemed to stretch all the way back to the occiput. A uniformed constable was seated at the bedside. The constable automatically checked the moment of recovered consciousness.

At that same moment in time, at North Division, Detective-Inspector James 'Jumbo' Collins was interrogating the drivers of the delivery van and the breakdown truck; a uniformed man sat in one corner with a pen and shorthand pad.

'Let's have that again, Mr . . . Mr . . .'

'Nick'll do, guv,' the delivery van driver said.

'Right, Nick.'

'Where from, guv?' Nick asked.

'Applying your brakes,' Collins said. He already had most of the picture, but another telling would implant it firmly and provide a confirmation of the notes already taken. 'You braked – when?'

'When the brown car braked,' Nick said reasonably. 'Else I'd've been right up his ring-piece.'

'And you saw the door of the parked car being . . .'

'Hang on, guv. No, I didn't really see the door opening at all. Must've been keeping my eyes on the Avenger. Seen his reds go on, like. So I braked. What I meant was that when I did have a look round, the Avenger was veering off to its right, see. Veered right and straight into the bus coming along Cartland Avenue. I reckoned the bloke was pissed.'

'And the parked car – let's try and get that straightened out,' Collins suggested.

'I seen its door was a bit open – not much. Then it shut again. That was about when the Avenger ploughed into the bus, like. Well, I heard that bloody great crunch and – naturally – I was looking at the pile-up.'

'You didn't see the parked car after that, you said,' Collins saw the van driver's head shake, and went to the other man. 'But you say you saw a car – which might have been the parked car in question – drive away, turn left and disappear down Cartland Avenue.'

'Yes, I did,' the breakdown driver agreed. 'But I was like Nick here. Fact is, I'm out of the waggon and out there across the road to give a hand with the pile-up. That's part of my job, sir. I wouldn't like to say it was the same car as you want to know about. All too sudden. For all I know it might have been a car coming along Cartland Avenue ahead of the bus. Nick's van's real big, arse-end on – and I was less than eight feet astern of him.'

Collins asked him : 'Been on the job long?'

'Seven years, sir.'

'Before that – the Navy?'

'Merchant Navy, yes – I . . . how'd you know that?'

'I'm a mind reader,' Collins growled at him. 'This car – what colour? Make? Size? Take your time.'

'Honest, sir, I haven't the foggiest idea. It was a dark-coloured job. Just a shape – dark – could've been anything between a family saloon to a limousine for all I know. But there was a car went on down the avenue when the crash happened.'

'All right,' Collins said. 'Constable!'

'Sir!' the shorthand writer stood up.

'Take these two chaps down to the canteen and see they have a drop of something or other. Look, you lads, I want you both to go down to our canteen and think it all over again. I don't want to keep you a moment longer than is necessary. Think about it, speak about it between yourselves. And let's have you back here in fifteen minutes.'

'Fair enough, guv,' Nick said agreeably. 'Wouldn't mind a drop of chai, myself. Right – see you later then.'

The telephone rang as they went out.

Collins lifted it.

'Inspector Collins, North Division.'

'Jack Lodge, Jumbo,' Steve Pearson's voice informed him. Jack Lodge was the editor of the city's leading evening paper.

'Okay, put him on, Steve.' He waited. 'Hello, Jack. How's the man?'

'Usual, Jumbo; not bad, not good, either. Do I hear the right strength on Tony Bolesco this morning?'

'Yes. But I can't give anything until the medical examiner's had a look at him.'

'It *is* fatal then?'

'Couldn't be more so. How long have you got?'

'For a column – until two o'clock at the latest. For a stopper – oh, about three-thirty.'

'Frank Wishart'll be here at two o'clock. I'll do my utmost to let him have something when he arrives. I suggest you ring in to Frank direct. Right?'

'Great, fine. Errm . . . Jumbo, is this apt to become . . .'

'I get that funny smell in the air, Jack.'

'Front-page stuff? I'm only asking for make-up purposes.'

'It almost certainly could be. Can't say more'n that.'

'Fine. Thanks a lot. Bye.'

Collins grunted in reply and replaced the phone. He pressed a button on a panel. Several seconds later Dusty Miller and

Slim Summerville entered the office. 'Sit down somewhere,' Collins told them.

The sergeant was of slighter build than usual for a policeman. He was wearing a sports jacket, corduroy trousers, wore his hair rather long, an outsize necktie and suède shoes. The girl was miniskirted, leather jacketed, very attractive, and carried a dinky umbrella and a chocolate brown fringed handbag. They seated themselves and waited.

'Slim,' Collins said to the girl, 'you were riding passenger. Did you see a car – any sort of vehicle – turning left and proceeding along Cartland Avenue when the crash occurred?'

'No, sir.'

'What were you doing when the crash occurred?'

'Looking at the Gas Board men with the pneumatic drills and trying to keep the din out of my head. In fact, I hardly heard the crash.'

'Well it can't be helped. You, Dusty?'

'I was watching the breakdown's jib. He didn't give me any warning at all. I was practically into him – less than five or six feet, anyway. I should have remembered the halt sign on Elleston. In fact, I did, really; but it came before I expected it.'

'One-way thoroughfare,' Collins reminded him.

'I'd have been right up there had there been sufficient room. The Gas Board types had cordoned off about four or five feet of roadway width right alongside me. Not a hope of getting through.'

'Ah,' Collins said. 'You were right about the cause of death.'

'I didn't think safety glass would have . . .'

'Three shots, all within a three-inch group; all fired while the Avenger was in motion. Estimated range – four to five feet. Very close, but real smart shooting for all that. Deliberate, and very fast.'

'And Harmon, chief?' Miller asked.

'He'll live. Haven't managed to establish yet whether the head wound was caused by a fourth shot or by impact against some part of the car at the moment of collision.'

'If . . . I mean, if you . . .'

'Yes, go on, Dusty.' Collins nodded at him.

'I'd say it was a stray shot. Why else would he have driven out . . .'

'I think so, too. We'll know when the team go over the car.'

'If we'd only been there behind them,' Miller said ruefully.

'As well you weren't. Chick Harmon's a smart laddie. Your orders were to keep at least one other vehicle . . .'

'We've have spotted that car, sir. Slim would, anyway. We'd have been a bit ahead of that Gas Board crowd, too. Someone we're looking for had it all worked out rather well, hadn't he?'

'Aye. Someone. Who're we looking for, Slim?' Collins asked her.

The girl thought about it. 'Could be an imported operator on a contract, sir. I can't think of any of the clients who could hit a *bus* with a pistol outside a range of ten yards. A professional – who's been moving out of the big centres?'

'Or who had a personal grudge against Bolesco sufficient to . . .' Miller began to suggest.

'Any and all of the South Side mobs for a start,' Collins said. 'It's a devil of a wide field to hunt over. Devilish wide.'

Collins lifted the telephone when it rang. 'Yes, right, Steve. Ah. Thanks – yes, I'll get over there after lunch.' He replaced the telephone and told them: 'Harmon's come round. It must have been a stray shot, according to what he's divulged.'

'He may have seen who fired . . .' Slim Summerville began.

'If he did, he isn't coming through with it.'

They hadn't expected that Harmon would. Made the job all the more frustrating. The Mafia termed it – Omerta.

At two-thirty that afternoon Frank Wishart released a Press statement to Jack Lodge whose first edition carried it in the

Stop Press front-page slot. In the Late Final it rated a half-column comment. It comprised an account of the collision, the names of the victims, and the location of the incident. The real cause of death remained a subject for conjecture, though several observers on the scene at the time, who had gone to the assistance of the Avenger's occupants, were aware of the neck wounds sustained by Tony Bolesco.

The account was read by some with relief, by others with regret, with hope, with hate, with satisfaction.

Detective-Constable Bill Baker and Jumbo Collins visited Chick Harmon in his special ward at three o'clock. The uniformed guard got off his chair and saluted the inspector smartly, and stood awaiting further orders. He was instructed to leave the ward, and Collins promptly began to seek information. Harmon's face was half-covered with bandages, and an aluminium splint had been applied to his right forearm, but he was sitting up and smoking his first cigarette since the crash.

'Hi, Jumbo,' Harmon said, pleasantly enough, extending the cigarette packet, which both policemen declined with a word of thanks. 'How's Tony making out?'

'Hard to tell, Chick,' Collins replied. 'Got a hard crack – you both did. How'd you come to veer into that bus, anyway?'

'I thought you'd have been able to tell me that.'

No one had told Harmon anything. Except for a physician, the ward sister and the uniformed guard, he'd seen no one, and they couldn't tell him a thing about it. They hadn't been there, had they? But they knew, for all that.

'Let's hear the details from when you drew alongside the stop sign on Cartland Avenue,' Collins suggested.

'I don't think I ever made it that far, Jumbo.'

'No? Why not?'

'There was all that glass flying about. I got a hell of a smack on the forehead and from then on I was in the clouds.'

'Is it right that you'd picked up Bolesco at . . .'

24

'Yeh, sure. I went up to the jail for him and took him back to town. Took him to visit his old man in hospital, you know.'

'Ah. The old man's pretty bad, I hear.'

Collins nodded as he spoke. Bolesco Senior had been a respectable citizen all his life. There wasn't a single entry against him in the books, nor against the late mother of the latest fatality. Good, hard-working parents, immigrants from southern Italy over thirty years earlier. As for the patient in the bed, he'd been convicted of a break-in and one case of assault and breach of the peace – namely, being involved in a street corner rammy after too much booze when two livelier clients had sustained minor injuries. Chick was a fly-man. He'd beaten a host of charges due to skilful representation, paid for by the Bolesco mob. Bolesco looked after his own when it came to the push, though, ironically enough, he hadn't had sufficient proof or skilful defence work in the courts to beat his own misdemeanour. Luck of the draw, perhaps – that's how Tony Bolesco would have viewed the set-up.

'Take anyone else back to town, Chick?' Collins asked.

'Tony gave . . .'

'Ah?'

'We took another boy back with us, yeh.'

'Would I know him?'

'Pat Lynch. Irish Pat.'

'I know him,' Collins said. 'Was he at the hospital with you?'

'We dropped him off at a bus-stop when we got into town,' Harmon said. 'It was just a favour on Tony's part. Him and Pat had been mates in there. Came out the same time, see?'

Irish Pat was a convicted gelly-man.

Collins asked: 'What did he chat about, Chick?'

'Who – Tony or Pat?'

'Let's say both.'

'Sex,' Harmon said, and with some truth.

'Anything else?'

25

'Not so far as I remember. All Pat wanted was a rub at the brush, see? Natural, after three years up the hill there.'

'You dropped him off and went to the hospital. Right, from the hospital – where?'

'Back to Elleston Road – to Tony's place.'

It all checked, so far as it went. Collins took his time. Bill Baker doodled with his pen on the writing pad, keeping his eyes down on what he was doing.

'The flying glass, you said.' Collins cleared his throat.

'Yeh. All over the front of the car.'

'What d'you think broke the window – or was it the windscreen?'

'The window, Jumbo. Must have been. The screen was clear.'

'Some kid heaving bricks, maybe?'

'I don't know. There was a mob of road-drillers working; but they were on the right side of the road. I've been wondering if it was a kind of freak chunk of stone, or something. But they were on the other side – behind us, too.'

'Your driving window – up or down?'

'Up. Right up tight. I remember that. I always have it closed up. Then there was this bloody crack in the face, and – I think it must have been my own blood – couldn't see a thing.'

'Not Tony's blood,' Collins suggested.

'Tony's – how could it have been? I remember he was leaning over on to me, that's all. You know, like you lean over if you're trying to get into your pocket, and that.'

'You were coming up to the stop sign – how fast were you ...'

Harmon sat up straighter in the bed. 'Now, wait a minute. I didn't think about it – until now. A mug had opened his driving door and I had to pull up.'

'What driving door, Chick?' Collins' eyes flickered towards Bill Baker's moving pen.

'A mug in a car – parked car, on my left. If I hadn't put

26

the anchors down I'd have taken his door off.' Harmon's un-injured arm rose and rested against his bandaged forehead. 'I haven't got round to thinking straight yet. I remember the door – opening a bit. Then the door closed again when he seen us coming up behind him. You get some crazy bastards in motors.'

'But you didn't see who he was. A woman, maybe,' Collins said.

'All I saw was the intersection ahead and the traffic in the mirror behind us, and that's all. Maybe Tony saw who it was. Didn't you ask him?'

'Haven't got round to asking him anything yet, Chick. He got a bad crack, as I said earlier on. I was hoping you might have been able to . . .'

'I didn't have a second to myself,' Harmon protested. 'We got past the parked car and then it all happened. Just when we were past the car.'

'And then you swerved right into the bus.'

'I couldn't see a bloody thing. I don't remember hitting the bus. Honest, Jumbo. Well, I think I sort of remember see-ing the bus – I must have passed out about then. Tony'll maybe be able to give you the strength from there.'

'He get any hard words when he was inside?' Collins asked.

'If he did, he didn't mention them, no.'

'Nobody you can think of who wanted him to . . .'

'I can think of a few, sure,' Harmon said quickly. 'He had enemies. We all have enemies. Why the question, anyway?'

Collins ignored the question. He said: 'Who's got the knife in him, Chick? Come on, come on.'

'After doing a stretch like that? How would I know? You don't make a lot of sense to me, Jumbo. You trying to tell me that smash was a . . .'

'I'm trying to find out,' Collins told him. 'He's a pal of yours, right?'

'About the best I ever knew, sure. I'd do anything for Tony.' Harmon reached out with his good arm, and his fingers jabbed into the big man's forearm. 'Look, Jumbo, if that was an attempt at knocking Tony . . .'

'You'd like to put the score level, right?'

'Right. Dead right.' Harmon nodded vehemently.

'Who was the mug in the parked car?'

'I've no idea!' Harmon protested. 'Honest to God. I'd tell you if I did . . . if he meant us to hit that bus.'

'I tell you something, Chick, if it'll make your brains work any better than they've been doing this far.'

'Go on, tell me. If that was meant to . . .'

Collins interrupted with: 'Who's travelling at the moment?'

'From where?'

'The south, for a start. Who's in town? I'm looking for a right hard boy now, Chick. Hard as they come. A contractor, maybe.'

'Jesus – who's got his name on the gate?' Harmon asked jerkily.

'Could be yours,' Collins said flatly.

'Mine – a contractor? I don't have . . .'

'You picked up Tony. You've got all that loot no one ever found. Right. Someone's interested, and has the means of finding out, now that Tony's been liberated.'

'I don't have any loot, chum,' Harmon retorted. 'Tony – okay. He knows where he put it. Fair enough. But I don't know. Anyway, who's going to try putting the arm on Tony in this town? Tell me that.'

'The mug in the parked car, Chick. Come on. boy – who is he?'

'You're kidding, Jumbo.'

Collins shook his head. 'Who's in town – who's travelling?'

'I can't think of anyone like a contractor. Look, this is daft, so it is. I'm not frightened, either. That's your form, right? Trying to scare me, okay?'

'I never scared you, Chick. Waste of good time. I am trying to preserve your good health, boy. That's my job.'

'I don't know of anybody from the south,' Harmon said flatly.

'Better make a point of finding out, boy. When you do, let me know. You know my phone number by this time.'

'Jesus, Jumbo – what's on your mind now?' Harmon asked irritably.

'Three shots,' Collins told him, 'in a real tight group – all three in Tony Bolesco's – the late Tony Bolesco's neck; that's what.'

But there was not the reaction he expected – simply disbelief.

Harmon was actually sneering.

Collins said: 'Bill, let's have those prints.'

Bill Baker had expected all of it. The Harmons of the world had to be convinced before they would talk. They always made a point of having a single card, albeit a low-numbered card in the deck, in their meagre reserve. The photographs might tempt them to lead it. He slipped the envelope of photographs out of his notepad and without saying a word handed them to the patient in the bed. Harmon looked at all three of them; at the full-length shot of the deceased on the slab, at the close-up of the victim's neck and face showing Bolesco's half-closed dead eyes and the punctures, at the close-up of the three missiles that had caused those same punctures.

Harmon returned them awkwardly to the envelope and handed it back to the detective-constable. The back of his uninjured hand went up to wipe off the starting perspiration from his upper lip and jaw.

'Who was it, Chick? Come on, come on,' Collins pressed him.

Harmon's head moved from side to side.

'You were both for it,' Collins reminded him. 'You caught the last one, the fourth shot. We'll find it in your car when we go over the vehicle.'

'Maybe,' Harmon admitted softly.

'We will. The right side windows weren't broken, despite

the dunt you hit that bus with. We'll find it, Chick. Who's got the finger on you?'

'Nobody, Jumbo. I'd know if there was. I'd get the tip.'

'You must've heard the shots.'

'I don't remember hearing anything. Just the glass – it came spraying all over the front of the car. Maybe I did hear shots – I can't remember hearing any, that's all. And that's a fact.'

'From a gun less than ten feet away?'

'There was all that rammy going on across the road. They had a couple of drills going. Come to that, we had the car radio on as well.'

Bill Baker winked across the patient's head at the inspector and nodded. The accident report confirmed the radio had survived the impact with the omnibus and that a screech of pop music had been audible when the rescue team had brought out the victims.

'So you didn't hear shots,' Collins muttered.

'I'd tell you if I had, Jumbo. Tony was right good to me. We hit it off right. We was chinas. I get the full strength of it now. The door opening; the road squad kicking up a row; me having to slow up as we passed him. Yeh, it was a professional. Okay, so some of the local opposition put a contract out. I agree with you. It must have been a contract. All that planning – the whole deal from the word go.'

'Who's putting the arm on the Bolesco . . .'

'Nobodys putting the arm on us. That's the truth. I'd know, wouldn't I?'

'I think you do know, Chick,' Collins persisted relentlessly. 'I think you'll have a go in reply when you get out of here, too.'

Harmon smiled thinly back at him. 'Because you say I was in the act when Vincent Duffy got his.'

'I said that?' Collins expressed astonishment. 'When, Chick?'

'Your tribe said it. Rimmer and that zombie Wishart. They said I was on the job. I wasn't. I can prove I wasn't.'

'You did, too – in court. But you *were* in on the job.' Collins made a happy beam of pleasure break out over his face. 'Best thing you ever did. Vincent Duffy'd been around far too long. The law says we can't hang him up from the beam nowadays; but you bright lads did the job for us. I'm happy, Chick. I'll give you a list of about a round dozen of the others to handle. That car, boy. What model?'

'I didn't really see it . . .'

'But you saw the driver's door opening. But you didn't really see the car. My goodness, how short-sighted can you get?'

'I didn't notice the model, I meant.'

'Colour then.'

'Dark colour. Could have been dark blue, bottle green; dark like that. Black, maybe, come to that.'

'Not so many black motors nowadays,' Collins reminded him. 'If it's black, we might have a chance. Think about it, Chick.'

'I've thought about it. I don't know!'

Collins was inclined to believe him. In all probability the car had been hoisted: one of the patrols would find it in an alley somewhere, abandoned.

'How's Nat MacDowell making out these days?' Collins asked.

Harmon paused before replying. 'Nat's fine.'

'When'd you see him last?'

'Last week. Aye, he's fine,' Harmon nodded as he spoke.

'Since last week – like yesterday, for example?'

'No, right enough, Jumbo. Never seen him since last week.' The patient in the bed began to smile thinly. 'Aye, I'm on your beam now. Me'n Nat working the contract between us, eh?'

'Eh?' Collins looked blankly down at him.

'Nat's a hard boy. Fair enough – we know that. But he's no mug.'

'Not when he's been running the mob since Tony went up the

hill,' Collins agreed. 'Long time like that – you begin to get ideas.'

'No,' Harmon said. 'No! That's the truth. Besides, Nat wouldn't know how to hold on to a gun right. Look – see them photographs you've got there?' Harmon's thumb jerked at Baker's notepad. 'See them? See them all placed like that. Our motor was on the move at the time – aye, supposing what you're telling me the truth, like. We was moving – slow, sure – but moving. It must have took a right sharp man with a short gun to place them in that neat.'

'Who, for instance, Chick?'

'Nobody I know about, Jumbo.'

'You've plenty of time to try and remember,' Collins told him. 'And you're staying in here until you do.'

'Oh, hey! Wait a minute – play the bloody game. I've a wife and two weans, and they like to see me . . .'

'No visitors, no phone calls, no mail,' Collins told him curtly. 'When you're fit to be discharged from here you go into Bellheath Hall.'

'So I'm to be on remand? What have I done?'

'You'll find out in the course of time. And,' Collins said, 'I know you're going to call in Laurence Dinnie – you're entitled to see your legal adviser – but Dinnie never cut any ice with me. I'll see you – when your mind clears.'

Collins and Baker drove back to North Division.

3

Duty Sergeant Steve Pearson observed their entry and, as Collins and Baker passed his counter, offered a file and several report forms. Baker nodded acknowledgement and took charge of the papers.

Collins asked: 'How many have we got this time?'

'Three, so far,' Steve Pearson answered wearily, yawning. He had two hours to do before knocking off, and he'd spent the majority of the morning of that day – during his official off-duty time – in a packed courtroom, giving professional evidence to a bored sheriff and a brace of verbal battlers in the shape of the procurator fiscal and the defence counsel. The first of the nuts had arrived to confess to the murder of the late Anthony Bolesco. Steve counted them off on his fingers. 'One – Gregory Hamilton; two – Torquil Ossian Mac-Kaskill; three – James Craig Rose . . . and Benjie Booth, of course.'

'How'd Benjie kill this time?' Collins asked steadily, his mind on a previous case for investigation.

'Same way he killed them two clients last month,' Pearson told him evenly, stifling another yawn. 'A karate chop to the point of the jaw, and then the boot in the lower ribs when he was down. Take a duffy at the lower panel of my counter.'

Collins surveyed the indentations on the counter front. 'Tut, tut, Benjie's right worked up.'

'High's a chinkee kite,' Pearson agreed.

'Might be he could – see you later, Steve,' Collins muttered. 'I'll take Benjie first – three minutes.'

'Three minutes, Jumbo,' the sergeant confirmed, slightly surprised.

Collins let his tongue play in a cavity between his teeth as he went into his office. One had to go through the same routine all the time, and every time. There might come the day when the poor deranged brain of Benjie Booth might choose to make the grotesque imagination bear the most horrifying form of fruit. Despite his age and physique Benjie Booth was sufficiently strong to strangle some infirm victim in a sudden brainstorm of frenzy. The head-shrinkers had pronounced him harmless on several occasions, so he was free to roam the streets. At the same time, with a little gentle prodding, Benjie could be persuaded to supply information, if not of an accurate nature, then with another strength on which to act accordingly.

Collins pressed a bell on his desk and was scanning the file on his agenda when a uniformed constable ushered in Benjie and then took a chair beside the office door.

'Hello, Benjie; how's the boy?' Collins said, smiling at the little man across the desk from him.

'Orra boys, Jumbo. Orra boys. How's yoursel', eh?' Benjie screwed up his face and let Collins see his broken stained teeth. His hands hovered in the air in front of him, the fingers and thumbs working in the strange manner of the modern pop-singer.

'For a fag, Benjie?'

'You're a Christian man, Jumbo, so you are.' Benjie reached for the packet and helped himself to a cigarette, and took a second which he tucked into his breast pocket. From a pocket he produced a match and struck it against the desk. 'Been a rare day, eh, Jumbo?'

'Great. What brings you in tonight, boy?'

'The big fellah no' tell you?'

'Not yet. What's on then? Come to tell me something?'

'Sing you a song, Jumbo.'

'A new one, maybe?'

'A right brammer, so it is. Here's it here.' Benjie began to sing, to the tune of 'Come Back to Sorrento': 'D'ya see them

queuein' fur fish suppers . . . High fish tea and bread an' butter
. . . Drunken baaastards inna gutter . . . Ah don't like Saltcoats arra Fair – ahh.'

'Some song that, Benjie,' Collins said, aware of the attendant
constable's open despair by the door.

'Second verse – comin' up,' Benjie announced proudly,
taking on a lungful of smoke and exhaling before rendering:
'What a day we had at Saltcoats . . . And our presents had
been bought – ahh . . . A stalk of rock for my old Aunt Fanny
. . . And a salt dish fur ma Mammy.' Benjie cleared his throat
and sprang into the chorus: 'Saltcoeeetes – goodbye!
I hate the smell of your rotten seaweed . . . Ne'er again I'll
ever see youse . . . Auld – Saltacoeetes . . . goooda byee!'

Collins nodded solemn appreciation. 'That's great. You'll
get a booking for the Empire in no time at all, boy. I'm very
impressed. I really am. You get better and better.'

'Ach, you're just kiddin' me, Jumbo. Mind you, I used to be
a rare wee warbler in my time, so I did.'

'In the boxing ring as well, eh, Benjie?'

The little man jumped to his feet, indulging in a show of
shadow boxing. 'Benjie's the wee boy. Youse could hear them
shouting that – Benjie Booth's the wee boy.'

'You were the greatest of your time,' Collins said.

'Benjie was the greatest,' the little man crowed, dodging,
ducking and sparring at the air.

'Didn't I see you last night?' Collins said casually.

Benjie paused, dropping his fists, going back to the chair.
'Where was that, Jumbo?'

'Thought I noticed you down by the dog-track. Maybe I
was mistaken.'

'Not me, Jumbo. I never goes near the track. No money,
see?' He glanced at the immobile constable at the door. 'I just
went for a wee run round the block – keeping fit for the big
fight, eh?'

'Aye, you're right. Best thing – keeping fit. Wish I could do
the same,' Collins admitted. 'Ages since I had a glove on.'

'Rests the brain and exercises the body at the same time, Jumbo.'

'Sure. Like road work. Couple of miles is great.' Collins nodded as he spoke. 'See anything interesting, round the block?'

'No. I never see nothing. I just runs. Orra time.'

'With your eyes closed, likely, eh?'

'I'm no' looking fur trouble, Jumbo.'

Collins nodded again. 'How'd you fix Bolesco, Benjie?'

'Auld karate chop.' The little man's right hand chopped down on the desk surface. 'Wham! Just like that. Ha, eh? Wham!' Another chop. 'Straight in – just like that – once, twice – no bother at all.'

'Took a couple to put him down? You can do better than that, boy.' Collins said in a tone of disappointment.

'Then the boot – once, twice – straight in – just like that. And one fur luck.' Benjie's boot crashed against the desk upright, shaking the item of furniture visibly.

'Where'd it happen?'

'Eh?'

'Where'd it happen? When you downed Bolesco.'

'I don't remember, Jumbo,' Benjie admitted blankly, his eyes straying in the direction of the constable as if for confirmation.

'In the boozer, maybe, Benjie?'

'Inna boozer . . . so it was. Inna boozer, Jumbo. He comes out – into the close, like; and I creeps up behind him and – wham! Just like that. Once, twice – just like that. The big hammer – inna neck and jaw. Wham!'

'When you were going round the block last night, Benjie . . . what colour was that van in Rowan Street?'

'Wham – just like that . . . eh? What colour – the car? Big car?'

'Aye, the big car,' Collins nodded, eyeing the constable who produced a notepad and a pencil. 'What colour was the big car, boy?'

'I never seen no car, Jumbo. Never seen nothing round the block.'

'Same colour as this, maybe?' Collins produced a currency note from a drawer. 'Sort of light green, eh?'

'Black, Jumbo. Right dead black, so it was.' Benjie's eyes followed the gentle movement of the currency note as Collins waved it gently to and fro. 'Eh, Jumbo? Eh?'

'Here, put it in your pocket. I don't need it. I've got more in here.' Collins reached into the drawer and began to count a sheaf of notes with remote interest, and then returned them to the drawer, closing it.

'Ta, Jumbo. You're a Christian, so you are.'

'Black car – see the make?'

'No. I never seen nothing.'

'That's a terrible pity, Benjie. Oh, well, if you're not need-ing . . .'

'It was a Austin, Jumbo,' Benjie said quickly, as Collins made to rise from his chair.

'An Austin? How d'you make that out?'

'Seen it wrote onna front orra radiator, Jumbo. Bobby gived me a run home in't, once, like.'

'Bobby Whitehead?'

Benjie's jaw dropped slackly. 'I don't remember.'

'You never saw Bobby,' Collins suggested. 'You're just tell-ing me a lot of daft stories, eh? And here's me giving you Ready for a drink. I don't like my friends treating me like that, Benjie. It's not fair.'

'I keep on forgetting, Jumbo.'

'Aye, me too. Pity – great pity.' Collins opened the drawer and removed the money from it to his pocket.

'See the boy there, Jumbo?' Benjie said quickly.

'Who's the boy?'

'Bobby Whitehead, Jumbo.'

'Oh, aye, sure. What about him?'

'Selling the Blue Fliers. Him and Sammy Rankin. Blue Fliers. I seen them do it. Aye, last night – inna boozer.'

'Buy any yourself, maybe?'

'Not me. I'm not daft. them things kill you. Me – keep fit, me.'

'You're right, too.'

'And youse need a needle fur to stick the other stuff into your arm.'

'You know, Benjie, I've heard about that,' Collins admitted very confidentially. 'Never seen it done, mind; but they say it's just a wee bit jab in the arm and then a . . .'

'They can buy it inna Round Square Club in Blantyre Avenue,' Benjie whispered, leaning closer to Collins as the words emerged.

'That a fact? You're not telling me a lot of funny wee jokes . . .'

'Honest, Jumbo. Sure as death. Here, what about another sheet . . .'

'Let's hear another verse of that fine song, eh?' Collins grinned.

The little man began to work his fingers and thumbs again, his head weaving as his addled brain sought the words; and then: 'Ye see ra boat gaun doon ra watter . . . Ya see ra baggie minnows scatter . . . Weel they ken what we are after . . . Oor jeeley jaurs an' net in haun-ah. Saltcoeetes goodabyee . . .'

By then the attendant constable had taken action on his superior's nod. He caught Benjie by the arm as the little man was inhaling for the remainder for the chorus. 'Come on, Benjie lad – time we went.'

'Hey!'

'Time to go for a drink, boy,' the constable said.

'Hey, Jumbo! Here, what about another sheet, eh?'

'Sergeant Pearson's got a parcel for you in the charge-room,' Collins told him. 'Ask him for it on the way out. I'll see you.'

'Ya bastard, Jumbo Collins. Ya dirty big pig's bastard!'

'Come on, lad,' the constable said, tightening his grip.

'You watch it, Benjie,' Collins told him, 'else I'll have that sheet . . .'

'Ya couldn'a knock the top off an egg.'

'Tell Sergeant Pearson to give him the price of a drink, constable; and I want to see the sergeant in here as soon as it's convenient.'

'Yes, sir. Come on, you.'

'Dirty lotta pig's bastards . . . Saltcoeetes goodabyee . . . I hate you dirty rotten bastards . . .' Benjie sang as he was hustled out.

The office door closed behind them.

Collins sighed and devoted himself to thought.

When Steve Pearson answered the relayed summons, Collins was thinking about the Round Square Club. So far as he was immediately aware, no action had ever been taken against that establishment. 'Shut the door, Steve.'

The sergeant complied and waited.

'Robert Tullo Whitehead,' Collins muttered; and added: 'Eighteen Rowan Street . . . I think.'

'That's the number, right enough.'

'Fix a warrant and see Frank Wishart. I suggest a visit there – do the garage first – about four o'clock in the morning. Keep it soft and not too many men on the job. I'm looking for a bale of carpets.'

'And coats,' Pearson said. 'I've got the list.'

Collins nodded thoughtfully. 'See if you can get hold of Pixie Greer at Central, would you, Steve? That Round Square Club's worth a look over.'

'Oh hoh? Junk again?'

'No harm in having a look at it.'

'First time, far's I can recollect, Jumbo.'

'Aye, I know. Who's on the board of promoters there; any idea?'

'Chick Harmon, for one. I can check.'

'Is he now? That might be something. Listed as a company?'

'Of course. I'll get on to City Chambers. They'll have it.'

'See if you can get Pixie on the blower for me.'

Pearson nodded and let himself out of the office.

Collins called after him: 'I'll have the next sinful confessor in.'

'That's James Craig Rose. Bill Baker's dealing with the other two.'

'Good enough,' Collins said, thinking about the Round Square Club, and about Pixie Greer.

Pixie had been born with the christian names of Philemon Dixie Dean, which at school had developed into numerous obscene denominations, of which a few had developed into Pixie. At the age of thirty-one he had, after a variety of part-time jobs, been accepted into the force because of a signal act of good citizenship that had resulted in the apprehension of a ring of drug pushers. He was exactly five feet four inches in height, eight stone three pounds in weight, looked rather like a dissipated jockey, was a total abstainer and non-smoker, held a Third Dan in Judo, and had passed a very advanced course in the chemistry of narcotics with unprecedented distinction. On the job, he was known as – the Ferret.

Collins explored the cavity in his teeth, nodding absently.

In the interrogation room at the end of the corridor, Bill Baker watched an aged gentleman being ushered towards the chair at the other side of the square, bare unvarnished table at which he sat. The attendant constable drew out the other chair and the old man sat down.

The constable announced: 'Mr. MacKaskill.'

'My name's Baker, Mr. MacKaskill,' Bill Baker explained. 'I hear you would like to volunteer some information that might help us in our ...'

'I am here to answer in the name of ... The Lord,' the old man proclaimed in a fine west highland voice.

'I'm very glad to hear that, sir,' Baker said in a friendly voice.

'It is the Lord's will. It is that, indeed.'

'Well, yes, that's fine. Make yourself quite comfortable, sir.' Baker weighed up the cadaverous face and the protuberant eyes, and nodded at the attendant constable, who seated himself and searched for a pencil. 'Now then, sir, what is it you'd like to tell me? Take your time.'

'When the Lord made time, He made plenty of it, young man.'

'Er . . . yes, He certainly did just that, sir.'

'I have come . . . to confess.'

'I see, sir. About − that is, what is it you'd like to confess?'

'To striking down an evil sinner!'

Bill Baker braced himself like an infantryman about to advance upon a stubborn objective. They came in all shapes, sizes and ages. But it was essential that they be dealt with to the best of one's limited ability. The mentally disturbed were so frequently the most difficult of all clients in the trade. Religion, like strong drink, Baker reflected with regret, was often a very terrible thing. He cleared his throat and said: 'This is apt to be an evil world in certain respects, Mr. MacKaskill. As a policeman I have good reason for making that statement as I'm sure you'll appreciate.'

'A world of whores and fornicators!'

'I'm afraid that is often very true, sir.'

'*Tha an rathad cumhann, ach gabnaidh mi am fear rathad . . .*'

Baker interrupted discreetly with: 'You have the advantage of me, Mr. MacKaskill. I don't have the facility of the Gaelic, sir.'

'It is not gaylick, at all: it is . . . ghaalik!'

'I hasten to apologize. Now, if we can . . .'

'It was my own fault, Mr. Baker,' the old man admitted in a voice of doom and frank despair. 'I am truly repentant.'

'All you have to do is to tell me what happened, sir. That's all. Where it happened, and why.'

'It is bad job of work I had to do this day. It is that.'

41

'I'm sure it must have been. Let's begin with the time, shall we?' Bill Baker ran a finger round his tightening shirt collar.

'At five o'clock this day – I took the word of the Lord – and struck!'

'You're sure about the time, sir. It's rather important.'

'It was at five o'clock.'

'Good. Now then, you were at . . . where?'

'I crept up behind him, you see . . .'

Baker listened. The shots that had killed Tony Bolesco had been fired at very close range. Although all this wasn't making very much sense to him, MacKaskill just could have been the driver of the stationary car.

'Yes, sir. You were very close to him and . . .'

'It was terrible easy for a man like myself. As a boy in my own hills I used to stalk the stags. It was so easy for me.'

'Yes . . . ?'

'And when I got close behind him, I picked up the iron bar, and I smote the whoremongering Philistine down on his knees!' The old man rose from his chair and his right arm swept down in an incredibly fast arc of movement, so fast indeed that the attendant constable was on his feet and advancing upon him automatically. Baker waved him back. 'And I smote him again, on the back of his head and the back of his back as well.'

'With very great force, yes. I can see that, sir,' Bill Baker said with an effort towards decorum and patience he couldn't honestly feel. 'The iron bar, sir. Am I to understand you brought it with you? For this specific purpose of striking down such a sinner?'

'I picked it up, I told you. And don't you be going and trying to put words into my mouth like that, young man. I found it in my hand – an instrument of the Lord. It was there,' the old man explained distantly to the walls of the interrogation room, 'there – in my right hand.'

'But – that is,' Bill Baker suggested, weary of the interview, knowing there was nothing coming through of any value,

42

'you didn't mention whether you went into this public house where the deceased was known to have...'

'I did not, young man. I never go into those evil places, for they are dens of sin and fornication. Rather that allow a single drop of that foul spirit to pass my lips ... I would *commit* fornication!'

'Thank you, sir. At least we seem to have cleared up a point about which there was some dubiety. You didn't enter the public house.' Bill Baker tried another tack. 'And what did you do with the iron bar, sir?'

'It was ... taken from me.'

'By whom, Mr. MacKaskill?'

'By ... an angel of the Lord. And it was consumed in the flames.'

'The ... flames?'

'The sons of Aaron took either from them his censer, and put fire therein. And there went out fire from the Lord, and devoured them. The iron bar was devoured by the fire of the Lord.'

'I see, Mr. MacKaskill. That's what I ...'

'And the priest shall sprinkle the blood upon the altar of the Lord at the door of the tabernacle of the congregation, and burn the fat for a sweet savour unto the Lord. And they shall go forth ...'

'Mr. MacKaskill!' Baker jerked his head towards the constable.

'... and no more offer their sacrifices unto devils, after whom they have gone a-whoring. Therefore I said unto the children of Israel – no soul of you shall eat the blood, neither shall any stranger of you that journeyeth ...'

They had got him on his feet and were steering him out of the interrogation room with difficulty.

'... and amongst you eat blood! Therefore ye defile not yourselves therein! *I* am your Lord God!'

Another uniformed man relieved Bill Baker who, quivering slightly, made his way through to the charge room where

Sergeant Pearson was listening to the distant oration with profound interest. 'My God, Steve, we certainly get them in here after a killing, don't we?'

'Makes the job worthwhile, Bill laddie. Wait'll you've been on it as long as I have, matey.' Pearson chuckled as he spoke, then laughed.

'Said he would rather commit fornication than enjoy a decent dram,' Baker informed the sympathetic sergeant.

'At *his* age? Must be eighty if he's a day. Must be real nice to have the choice, I'd say. Isn't life wonderful – if you manage to live that long?'

'Jesus P. J. Christ,' Bill Baker muttered with heartfelt relief. 'Who's next for the chop; or is Jumbo taking him on?'

'Jumbo's got a bloke called Rose. Your next client's called Gregory Hamilton.'

'Do we know him, Steve?' Baker asked hopefully. With a known client, life became easier.

'Not yet; not yet, anyway, Bill.'

'Heaven preserve me, and my patience then. Let's have him in.'

4

The waitress in the café across the street from the entrance to North Division Headquarters noticed the young couple coming in and bided her time to let them settle into the warmth of the place after the sleeting rain of the streets. The man was about twenty-five, the waitress thought; the girl about twenty. Both were quietly dressed and tidy, and with an air of genteel respect despite the haggard expressions on their faces. The waitress sighed, remembering that anyone could make mistakes. She herself had been obliged to face the altar at eighteen when she'd been three months gone. It happened every day. Anyone, even the most genteel, could be forgetful and consequently regretful.

Eventually the waitress picked up a menu and approached their table.

'Good evening, sir,' she said briskly. 'Nasty night again.'

The young man mumbled several sounds of what she took to be agreement.

'Care to take off your coat, sir? I'll just hang it on the . . .'

'Thanks no – good of you. Very kind. I'm . . . I'm not staying, you see. Could you . . .' The young man broke off and glanced at the girl's face for several seconds before going on. 'Could you fetch a pot of tea, please?'

'For two, sir?'

'Well, I – you see . . .'

'I think you should, Bert,' the girl said to him. 'Yes,' she said to the waitress, 'for two, please.'

'Anything to eat, miss? We do our own home-baking here.'

'No, I – I don't really think I could eat anything.' The girl

45

sniffed and touched her face with a wisp of handkerchief.

'Something the matter, miss?' the waitress asked with genuine concern. 'Like to go to the ladies' room. I'll show you – just across . . .'

'I'll be all right in a minute.' The girl smiled back at her, making a great effort. 'Just a spot of . . . of the cold.'

'It's right bitter out,' the waitress said. 'I won't be long, sir.'

She heard their mumble of thanks as she went back to the serving hatch and gave the order, then turned slowly, making a note on her pad, and watching them at the table, their heads within a few inches of each other. The world, the waitress reflected, revolved round two things – money and sex. Eyeing their clothes, the quality of their shoes, and the delicate watch on the girl's left wrist, the waitress decided it must be sex. But the kid didn't look as if she was expecting. Maybe she'd just missed her turn and was panicking over it unnecessarily.

But the waitress was wrong on both counts.

The couple's problem was more serious than that.

Their problem was murder.

The girl whispered: 'I'm so frightened, Bert.'

'We're agreed on it. I'm frightened, too; been frightened for four years. But we're – you're still in the same frame of mind . . .'

'Of course. But I still think we ought to have consulted a solicitor before coming here. Even if only to ask why . . .'

'What's the use of a solicitor now? I'm guilty. I've been trying to live with that all this time. What's the point?'

'A solicitor would be able to advise you on – he'd be able to afford you some sort of protection – even if it's only protection against yourself, Bert. It isn't too late to go and make an appointment.'

'Better if you came over nearer to the radiator, miss,' the waitress said as she arranged the table-top for them. 'It's the door, you know. Keeps blowing open and shut with the wind. The latch's broken again.'

'I'm not really cold, thank you all the same. Perhaps I will . . . later, though.'

'Sure you wouldn't like something to eat, miss? Sir?'

The young man shook his head. 'You'd better have something, Helen. I may be some time across the way.' He said to the waitress: 'Let's have some scones, or something, please. With butter and jam.'

'Yes, sir. Strawberry?'

'That'd be fine, thanks.' He turned towards the girl again, pausing until the waitress was back at the serving hatch. 'I'll ask them to come and let you know . . . if – if they – they'll have to, of course.'

'Yes, I suppose they will, Bert. But they'll allow you visitors . . . won't they? Look, let me go and find someone in the morning. You're entitled to legal advice. I heard my father saying that, once. I'm sure he said a prisoner was entitled to have a solicitor present during . . .'

'I don't want a solicitor, Helen,' the young man told her jerkily. He sat back in his chair and looked round the café. Three workmen were hunched over a table near the serving hatch, smoking and discussing some sort of plan they'd spread on the table between them. An elderly woman was reading an evening newspaper in a corner, oblivious of everything but the column she held too close to her aged eyes. A couple of teenagers were holding hands and listening to the canned music that was emanating from some speaker near the ceiling. A gust of cold air swept through the place as a man carrying a baker's tray entered from the street. Everyone else was so uncomplicated, the young man thought, watching the waitress coming back with a plate and some cutlery. 'She's coming back.'

'I can see her in the mirror,' the girl said.

He thanked the waitress and paid for the service, giving her a generous tip that brought out a gasp of thanks. The nagging fear had suddenly gone out of him; it was like waiting in the dentist's chair for the first rasp of the drill, and now the time had come for the amalgam and the filling. 'Helen,' he said, gulping at the tea, 'I – if I don't go now ...'

'Please, Bert, at least finish your tea.' The girl sniffed and shook her head, making an effort at a smile. 'Silly sort of thing to say. I don't quite know what I'm saying. Wouldn't it be better if I were to come with you? Please, Bert.'

'They'd find a way of implicating you.'

'But that's impossible!'

'Not with them. I'm going, darling. I'll ask them to send someone ...'

'I'll come across later and ...'

'Now, Helen, that's just not on. Promise. Stay until some-one ...'

'All right. I'll stay—promise. Kiss me, Bert.'

He did, hurriedly, barely touching her lips and cheek – and then he got up and crossed the street to walk into the forbidding entrance of North Division Headquarters.

In his office Jumbo Collins was having considerable difficulty in making up his mind about James Craig Rose. He had established that the client's name was James Craig Rose, that he was fifty-two years old, and that he resided at eighteen King Harald Street, during which time he had been able to assess the fact that Rose wasn't short of finances, if his coat, suit, shirt, shoes and wristlet watch were immediately reflected in a monetary sense. Collins read over the notes he had taken, pursed his lips and let his tongue explore the cavity between his teeth.

'One more item, sir – telephone number?'

'Never use the beastly things, Inspector,' Rose told him in a slightly simpering voice.

'Right then. So you wanted to tell me all about it.'

'You haven't asked me my profession, Inspector,' Rose objected.

'Does that seem to you to be relevant in this instance, sir?'

48

'It would be for you to decide.'

'What is your profession, Mr. Rose?' Collins asked patiently, catching the eye of the attendant constable behind the latest client. The constable poised his pencil above his pad. 'Or vocation?'

Rose smiled and made a small sound in his throat. 'I'm a company director, Inspector.'

'Thank you, sir. Company director. Right.'

'I hold the controlling interest in De Crespigny Holdings, forty-two per cent of the stock in Calliferton Engineering, and just over a quarter of the stock of Ingerwell Electrics.'

The obvious observation was 'Congratulations', Collins thought; but said: 'That's very satisfactory, sir; thank you. Now then – let's get . . .'

'And I'm on the board of South City Securities, too.'

'That's very useful, sir. Tell me, what connection did you have with the deceased; Anthony Bolesco?'

'None whatsoever, Inspector. He was simply someone who had to be liquidated. I felt it to be my . . .'

'Mister Rose, one doesn't feel it to be one's duty to exterminate one's fellow human beings. Not in this country, anyway.'

'I did,' Rose said firmly.

'And you'd had this intention for some time, right?'

'Hmmm. Years and years. The man was a menace to society.'

'What gave you that idea, Mr. Rose?'

'Everyone knew what sort of swine Bolesco was. One has only to read the newspapers to . . .'

'Let's get round to the preparation you put into this undertaking.' Collins glanced at the clock on the wall. 'After all, to make a success of this must have necessitated a great deal of thoughtful planning.'

'And money, Inspector,' Rose said, smirking smugly.

'Of which you have adequate resources, of course.'

'Hmmm, oodles of it, yes. You must come round and see

49

my flat, you know. Rodney makes the most scrumptious cocktails.'

'I'm an abstainer, Mr. Rose. You mentioned Rodney – your brother?'

'My man, Inspector. Marvellous with coffee, too. Quite the most lovely man. Rodney would love having you.'

Collins stared pointedly at the young constable who, when he looked up from having taken the note, promptly straightened out his face and returned the deadpan expression of his superior. At that moment the telephone shrilled on the desk. Collins picked it up. 'Inspector Coll . . . oh, hello, Steve.'

Steve Pearson said over the line: 'Pixie Greer's on leave, Jumbo. Want me to put Slim and Dusty on the Round Square midden?'

'No, leave it meanwhile. Anything else?'

'Aye, there's a fellah just came in wants to chat you up. Says his name's Albert Younger.'

'Ah?'

'Come to give information to a mur . . .'

'Another, Steve?' Collins breathed heavily and waited.

'Aye – no, I mean – not another regular – another murder, like. One three years back there.'

'Which one?'

'Hugo Villiers, so he says. We cleared that up between us, as you'll mind all too well. First killing we worked on together. Want me to get the file out on it?'

'Do that, yes. See you in ten minutes.' Collins glanced at the calendar on his desk thoughtfully. It ought to have been Friday the Thirteenth, but it wasn't. The world was full of oddballs, the Roses, the MacKaskills, the Benjie Booths – but there was a difference, some of them suffered from delayed action. Three years was a surprisingly long time for the twisted mind to get its rickety wheels working, that was all. With a pencil Collins wrote down: Albert Younger. 'See what's going on the subject, would you, Steve?'

'No form at all. I've checked with South and Central. Not a single word. Want me to get in touch with General?'

'No, leave it. I'll attend to it later. Hold.'

'Holding. He's in the waiting room with one of the boys.'

'Right. Thanks.' Collins slammed down the phone and breathed heavily again. 'Now then, Mr. Rose – let's hear how you killed Bolesco.'

'Killed, no; executed, yes, Inspector.'

Collins stiffened. 'Just as you wish, sir. What manner of weapon . . .'

'I shot him, of course.'

'I see,' Collins said, aware of the attendant constable's interest. Nothing had been released about the manner of death. Even Jack Lodge had not been informed. That would emerge in the morning, when the procurator fiscal decided upon his course of official action. 'What with, sir?'

'A gun, naturally, Inspector.' Again, the little smirk. 'A revolver I had especially for the purpose.'

'Calibre, make, type?'

'No idea, really. Service weapon. Revolver – six-shooter, as they say in the films.'

'How many shots did you fire?' Collins was getting rather fed-up of the charade, but one had to meet them halfway at least. Orders from the top. Hear them out, sort them out, show them out.

'Can't remember, actually, Inspector. About a couple – or three.'

'But you know you . . .'

'I'm a very good shot, Inspector,' Rose said modestly.

'You put in a lot of practice, I take it?'

'I'm a natural, Inspector.'

Like the John Waynes and the Lone Ranger and the Tom Mixes; Tom Mix was going back a bit, too. Television and Hollywood had a hell of a lot to answer for. A natural – with a pistol. Collins was a fair pistol shot himself. The statement could be proved, of course. The divisional range was less than half a mile distant. The weaponry instructor, Jack Roughead, was undoubtedly the top pistol marksman in the country. Even Jack Roughead couldn't be classed as a natural Jack, like every other professional, had to stick to very regular practice, every week, every day for that matter. It was like playing snooker and the great concertos.

'Yes, I see, Mr. Rose,' Collins said tolerantly. 'Perhaps we can fix the time of the – execution.'

'To a minute, yes. Ten-forty-five this morning.'

'Ten – forty-five. I see.' To the nearest hour, anyway, Collins allowed mentally, making another note for the sake of appearances. 'And, tell me, where were you when you fired the couple or three shots?'

'I was sitting in my car.'

'Were you now? Where – were you sitting in your car?'

'At the street corner, of course.'

'You've brought the – the revolver with you, I suppose.'

'Oh, don't be so silly, Inspector. I threw the gun in the river – naturally. At the North Bridge. No one saw me do it, of course.'

'Of course. One has to be so careful about these things.' Collins nodded, his eyes straying towards the constable by the door. 'Excuse me a moment, Mr. Rose. Won't be long.'

Rose smiled at him as he rose to leave the office.

In the charge room, Collins said to the duty sergeant: 'James Craig Rose, Steve. De Crespigny Holdings, Calliferton Engineering, Ingerwell Electrics . . .'

'My sister's man used to work at Ingerwells, Jumbo.'

'Rose reckons he's on the directorial board of all three. Send out somebody on that. All the strength he can get on Rose. Must be some medical history on him somewhere . . . give it priority.'

'Going to hold him?'

'Hardly see the point. See if you can get him in the company registry for a start. That ought to show us something.'

'Give me five minutes,' Steve Pearson said.

Detective-constable Bill Baker appeared beside them at the counter. 'I've seen Gregory Hamilton, sir.'

'Ah? Hamilton – aye, Hamilton,' Collins said. 'So?'

Baker shook his head, giving the inspector a file. 'We've had him in on four similar occasions. He's been in the care of local authority for two years, at Belton Hall. Only got out yesterday. His sister's been climbing the wall, looking for him. She took responsibility for his welfare.'

'She here, the sister?'

'She's at Central. I said I'd see what you had to say and get Superintendent Wishart to authorize appropriate action.'

'Okay, Bill. Go up and see Frank. Far's as I'm concerned we needn't hold Hamilton. What's he like?'

'Seventy-two, no record; except the four appearances in the past. Involved in a car crash in 1954; severe head and face injuries – I asked for a check. That's it at the back of the file.'

'How'd he kill Bolesco, Bill?'

'Strangulation, sir.'

'Dear, dear. Okay, see Frank and tell him we don't need the old boy's company in the meantime. And see that sister of his has a few kind words. Frank can handle that side.'

'Yes, sir. Right away.'

'How old's the sister, Bill?'

'Sixty-three, sir.'

'Ah. Okay, see him off.' Collins watched his assistant mount the stairway up to Frank Wishart's office and permitted himself a sigh. They couldn't really help it, he reflected. Might happen to anyone. Put a foot off the pavement and there it was – impact, injury, blood and snot, the wards, the ultimate result. He didn't feel angry: it was simply a part of life and living . . . and sometimes dying.

'Rose's named on Ingerwell, Jumbo. De Crespigny, too.'

'Okay, Steve. That's all I wanted.' Collins went back to his office. Before entering the corridor, he turned and instructed: 'We'll have that medical check-out, Steve. Just to keep ourselves on the right side. The P.F. may have some questions to ask about him.'

'It'll take time.'

'In the morning'll do, Steve. When d'you knock off?'

The duty sergeant consulted his watch. 'In ninety-five minutes, if Charger Steed's on time . . . as usual.'

'See you tomorrow. 'Night.'

'Some caper, mate. Good luck.'

Collins acknowledged with a wave of his hand as he turned again and moved down the corridor to his office, walking slowly, thoughtfully, picking at his lip. A uniformed man was approaching with a sheaf of documents in one hand and a walkie-talkie set in the other.

Collins said: 'Simmonds?'

'Yes, sir.'

'In a couple of minutes a client's coming out of my office. Name of James Craig Rose. I want to know where he goes and what he does from the moment he leaves the premises. Rimmer about?'

'He's in the locker-room, sir.'

'Give him my compliments and relay that order.'

The constable nodded and hurried back the way he'd come.

Collins chose to go to a window farther along the corridor and look down on to the street outside. The café across the street was filling up with shift workers for a carry-out of snacks on their particular ways. James Craig Rose . . . you never knew where they'd turn up, or when, or why.

And then he remembered the other deceased client; Hugo Villiers. Three years before Villiers had been discovered beside the body of a night-watchman in a warehouse yard near the river. The night-watchman had two small calibre bullets in his brain-box, and Villiers had sustained a broken neck. The pistol that had discharged the shots had been found near the body of Villiers, and the bold boy's dabs had been established on a number of the weapon's components. An open and shut job if ever there had been such a job. And now, some cream-dream had arrived on the premises to confess to the killing. After three years!

Collins changed his mind and went back into the charge room.

'Hey, Steve, that Villiers file you . . .'

'Here, it's here, Jumbo. I was having a keek through it.'

'I'll take it with me for old time's sake.' Collins signed the receipt book and returned the pen to Pearson. 'Must be all of three years back,' he observed thoughtfully.

'Three years, two months and a few days. Just on the romantic Eve of Hogmanay. Rain, sleet and snow, boozers bawling out in song on the rocky road to glory, and that bastard Villiers mows down an old man of seventy-three . . . and then falls off the warehouse roof and breaks his dirty bloody neck. Ergo – roll on the New Year.' Pearson stretched his arms and back. 'Any luck with the client in bye, eh?'

Collins looked at the duty sergeant speculatively. 'You never know.'

'Aha?' Pearson's eyebrows raised and dropped. 'Heard you say that before, mate. We're on, are we?'

'Can't make head nor tail of him.'

'Looked like a poof to me,' the sergeant offered.

'Might be. You can never tell – but I got that impression as well.'

'The medical report, if any, ought to answer that one.'

'Aye, maybe.' Collins slapped the Villiers file gently on the counter, staring at nothing in particular. 'I've got something, somewhere, but I can't bring it out. You might think about it, Steve.'

'About what?'

'Chick Harmon – Chick and Bolesco's mob. They're not daft. They've got money. They don't – the majority of them – flash it around. So what do they do with it? Invest?' Collins watched the sergeant's face, and discovered precisely nothing. Steve wasn't on the wavelength yet.

Steve asked: 'Invest – what in?'

55

'Ingerwell Electrics, Calliferton Engineering . . . they're all sound propositions at this moment in time. See if you can get on to somebody in the Exchange, Steve. Who d'you know?'

'I'll find someone. So James Craig Rose is for the . . .'

'Only a thought, Steve. Crime's getting bigger and bigger, more and more respectable. More fashionable. See what you can dig up?'

Pearson watched his superior turn away from the counter. Then he acknowledged: 'Aye, sure thing, Jumbo. I'll do that.'

Collins found Rimmer loafing in the corridor. 'You all set, Dick?'

The lanky, sour-faced detective nodded without replying.

'He'll come through my door in a couple of minutes. I don't want him getting lost.'

'I've got two cars on the job. He won't get lost, sir.'

'Ring in when you see him settled.'

'I'll do that. Any real strength yet?'

Collins shook his head, paused at his office door, and then went in. Rose had taken a silk handkerchief out of his pocket and was holding it stretched between his hands, rather like a water-diviner with his twig. The attendant constable glanced up at Collins as he entered, shrugging in silent helplessness. Collins watched Rose allowing the handkerchief to slump in a bight between his hands, and then twirling it into a double-tapering cigar-shaped roll.

Rose looked up and, smirking, explained pontifically: 'In India the Thugee cult used to use silk scarves to perform their ritual executions. Black scarves which they kept tucked into their loin-cloths. When the rite had been performed, they indulged in prayer and proceeded to bury the body with curious steel axes. Tremendously interesting, really.'

Collins nodded and sat down. 'I remember seeing a film about it, Mr. Rose. Did you indulge in prayer before you shot Bolesco by any chance?'

'No, afterwards – like the Thugs. Immensely relaxing.'

From what he could recall of the macabre ritual, the Thugs spent many hours in prayer *before* they knocked off the poor victim, Collins reflected, putting the Villiers file into a drawer by his knee. He began to concentrate his gaze on Rose's hands. They looked surprisingly strong. And there were several long-healed scars across their backs. The scars looked like old burns, for the skin had never managed to lose a strikingly puckered appearance.

'Well, Mr. Rose, that'll be all in the meantime,' Collins said.

'Aren't you going to charge me, Inspector?' Rose smirked again.

'Until I check on a number of points, I'm not in a position to do that, sir. If you'd just step into the corridor the constable will . . .'

'You really mean that I can go? You see, I have to pick up Rodney.'

'Yes, you're free to leave, Mr. Rose,' Collins said, nodding.

'Aren't you going to look for the revolver?'

'Perhaps I will. In fact,' Collins said distantly, 'that might be quite a good idea.'

'You'd employ your frogmen, hmm?'

'That would be the general idea, sir.'

'May I come and watch? Would I be allowed to talk to your frogmen?'

'It would depend upon when we . . .'

'Oh, I could make any time available.' Rose smiled over his shoulder at the attendant constable. 'I've never had the pleasure of talking to a real frogman. And they look so handsome in those rubber suits, you know.'

Collins fought with himself for patience. 'I'll try and let you know when we will be searching the riverbed, sir.'

'Won't it take ages and ages?' Rose asked anxiously.

'Not if you're present to direct operations, sir.'

'Oh, golly, I'd love that, Inspector! I really would enjoy that.'

Collins rose and signed to the constable who went to open the office door. 'Well, that's it for the moment, sir,' he said heavily.

Rose followed the constable into the corridor. When the door had closed behind them, Collins sighed audibly. There were poofs and poofs, he reflected sadly, and they came in all shapes, colours, creeds and ages. But, and he felt utterly convinced, Rose wasn't a poof. He was possibly a damned good actor; but he wasn't a poof. There was none of that indescribable, revolting, murkiness about the man. Maybe he had missed it; even though he had tried to find it. It wasn't there – that shadiness, that sinister, repellent air he had so frequently sensed in the past when dealing with the homos.

The telephone on his desk rocked him back to procedure. 'Inspector Collins,' he said into the instrument.

'Forensic, sir. Sergeant Main here.'

'Hello, George. How's the man?'

'Think I've nailed down the rounds the doc removed from Bolesco, sir.'

'Why the doubt, George?'

'Haven't come across anything like this before, sir. With your approval I'd like to suggest they be sent to Metropolitan for comparison ... if possible.'

'We could always do that. Let's hear you then, George.'

'Japanese, sir. Nambu, I'd say – at a guess, that is.'

'Didn't we send you a Nambu last year? That kid with the collection of Samurai weapons over in Clintwood Gardens, if I remember. What's so weird about this lot?'

'Nambus normally run to eight millimetre. Point three-one calibre, near enough. Necked down cartridge cases; about a thousand feet per second at the muzzle, striking energy in the region of two-thirty foot pounds.'

'Aha. I seem to recall reading all that from your previous report, George. What's this then – you going to tell me they were fired from a sophisticated gas-gun or some new-fangled sort of cross-bow?'

George Main permitted himself a chuckle. 'No, sir, these were fired from a pistol. An automatic pistol, and a very rare model of same.'

'Now I'm listening, George. I like this a bit more. How rare?' Collins got a pencil working on his blotter. 'Let's have it nice and slowly now. Rare model of automatic pistol . . . right, go ahead.'

'I make this round to be approximately point two-eight-four inches in diameter. That settles it at seven millimetre.'

'Do we have anything of a similar calibre in Europe, George?'

'One I can think of immediately – the Mauser seven-by-fifty-seven. But that's a sporting *rifle* as a rule. The stalkers in the highlands like it for the stags.'

'Go on. How about the accommodating weapon?'

'It's been erroneously named as the Japanese Luger, but it's no more like a Luger in appearance than a three-eight Webley. It does, however, remind one of the Italian Glisenti. That's the gun we proved had finished off Danny Kruse about – what – two years . . .'

'I remember it. Fired it myself, in fact. Good unit,' Collins said rather impatiently. 'Keep it up, George,' he said, writing on the blotter. 'Can you furnish us with a picture; photostat copy from somewhere?'

'I've got that laid on, from one of our weaponry volumes.'

'I'd like one as soon as you can.'

'One's on its way by now. If I might repeat it, sir – I'm not entirely certain about this. If we could get a comparison from London I'd be much happier.'

'I can arrange that authority and draft a request.' Collins was beginning to feel quite happy with this information. 'Right, George, so we're looking for a Jap pistol . . . a souvenir . . . someone who has managed to get his hands on a rare small arm . . . collector type, d'you think?'

'An arms collector might pay a pretty good price for a seven mil Nambu, yes.' George Main then suggested: 'Could be the client's been out East at some time in his career. Wartime, possibly, I thought, sir.'

'I'm reading you very clearly, George. Right, boy, thanks a lot. I'll get the authority for comparison organized immediately. See you.'

'Bye, sir.' George Main hung up, leaving Collins gently swinging the telephone in his hand.

Bill Baker knocked and entered, looked at his superior, and dared to make a small encouraging smile. Ignoring the answering scowl, he asked: 'Yes? We're on to it, are we?'

'What gave you that ridiculous idea? What've you been on?'

'Getting shot of old Gregory Hamilton, sir. Superintendent Whishart cleared him as you suggested. I noticed another client in the waiting room.'

'Ah. Remember Hugo Villiers, Bill?'

'Naturally, sir. Don't say he's come back from the . . .'

'The client in the waiting room's come to confess to shooting the night watchman we found alongside him at the warehouses.'

'Great. Public co-operation's getting better and better.' Baker managed to read Collins' script on the blotter from his side of the desk, upside down though it was. He said: 'Nambu pistol, very rare model. Oh?'

'Ah. Very rare, Bill. Very handy, if we can find it. It's the gun that knocked off Tony this morning, according to George Main at Forensic. What d'you reckon to that little lot, chum?'

'I feel quite hopeful, sir,' Baker beamed down upon the inspector.

'Hm. Let's have this fortune-teller in from the waiting room, Bill. Bring him in and stick around with a pencil.'

'Right away, sir.'

5

Rimmer sat in the driving seat of the blue Viva and watched Rose come down the three stone steps of North Division's entrance, trying at the same time to determine which of the seven adjacently parked vehicles might be the property of the client. Two plain-clothes men in a Cortina farther up the street might have been entertaining similar reflections. Rose walked the length of the street and stood waiting at the intersection. He was within fifteen feet of the Cortina. Rimmer started his engine and waited. To the man beside him in the Viva he said: 'Check on the blower with the other car, Bob.'

'Right. This is Carswell. Checking communication. Over.'

'We've got you, Robbie. Looks like he's waiting for somebody to pick him up,' was the reply. 'We're all set to go. Over.'

'Could be. Keep your line clear. Over.'

'Roger. Out.'

They waited for several minutes. They watched Rose consult his wrist-watch, and then noted that he looked back along the street as if expecting to be followed. Then Rose stuck his hands deep into the pockets of his coat and, turning the corner, began to walk slowly along the main thoroughfare in an easterly direction. The Cortina began to get into motion, paused to allow the traffic to clear, and then turned after the client. The Viva moved up to the intersection smartly.

Rimmer nodded his head. His companion spoke into the walkie-talkie urgently. The Cortina team still had Rose in view. The Viva moved into the main thoroughfare and found a space at the kerb where Rimmer drew in and let the engine idle. The Cortina was about two hundred yards ahead, similarly parked in another space. Rose continued to walk leisurely on, and was about a further two hundred yards ahead of the Ford.

Suddenly his hand shot up and a cruising taxi drew up alongside of him.

As the client was climbing aboard the taxi the Cortina moved up behind the vehicle until the crew could clearly distinguish the number. It was relayed back to Rimmer in the Viva. The sour-faced detective made a note of it and watched the taxi draw away into the traffic stream. Then he wrote on the pad: 'Check whether James Craig Rose holds a driving licence.' It was an afterthought. Some of the big business types indulged themselves in flash motors until they finally found one that was too much for them and conveniently smashed it, and themselves into the bargain, thus eliminating a traffic danger. Others employed chauffeurs, professing that driving was a crashing bore, saving themselves physical injury and being picked up on a Section Six after a boozy party.

Rimmer got the Viva into motion and closed up on the Cortina.

Seven minutes later Rimmer reported to North Division: 'Subject proceeded by taxi to number eighteen King Harald Street, arriving there at nineteen hundred forty hours.'

'Hold,' the receiver ordered.

'Holding,' Rimmer acknowledged. He lit a cigarette and stared at the imposing terrace of Georgian houses that formed a fish-hook curve at the eastern end of the quiet street. There was a heap of loot here, all round him, Rimmer decided, sucking at the cigarette. The ironmongery parked at the kerb was ample confirmation of this. Nothing under three litres, nothing older than a nap of years. Nice, comfortable, smug, superior. At any moment some old cat would appear with her poodle on a gold chain and Russian sable coat. Rimmer waited, bored, a trifle disappointed.

'This I like,' his companion said wistfully. 'I've always wanted to live in the style in which I think I'd like to be accustomed, Dick.'

'You go on like that and they'll have you for a telly script-writer, china. In which you think you'd like to be accustomed – Christo!'

'Nice, though. See that Merc there – that's worth three and a half thousand. And I wouldn't say no to . . .'

'Cut it,' Rimmer snapped. 'Hello, yes – I'm getting you fine. Over.'

'Come on in, Dick.'

'Now? Both crews? Over.'

'Both crews,' the caller confirmed.

'Coming in,' Rimmer said. Into the walkie-talkie he said: 'Right, you two commandos, we're going home. Over.'

'Already? What about . . .'

'Already. What d'you think you're on, anyway? Looking for a C.B.E. or something? Over.'

'I could do with a pint for a start, Dick. Keep your crummy gongs. Over.'

'A pint,' Rimmer said thoughtfully. To his companion he asked : 'Who's nearest from here, Bob?'

'Dunky Jackson's. I'm on if they're paying.'

'Dunky Jackson's,' Rimmer transmitted. 'And you're paying. Over.'

'Your prick's got knotted, chum. Okay – Dunky's. Out.'

Rimmer sighed and looked along the terrace of sumptuous homes. He tossed the neat instrument into the door pocket and lit another cigarette. After a second glance at number eighteen, he engaged gear, muttered, and got the Viva headed in the direction of Dunky Jackson's hostelry.

An unexpected gust of light rain blurred the windscreen.

Jumbo Collins studied the appended note that Steve Pearson had included with the Hugo Villers file. It ran: 'Albert Younger, British, white, twenty-five years, born in Belfast. Residence Nine Greenfield Gardens. No trace of Criminal Record immediately available.'

The inspector didn't need to be reminded of Villiers. There were clients and clients; the misled, the near negative, the blatantly stupid, the minor offenders, those who were dealt with and partially forgotten until their names appeared once more on a charge sheet. There were the ingenious men, the cunning boys who provided something new, a few of them very likeable, the majority detestable. And there were the dregs, the rodents of society, the clients about whom there was precisely nothing that a well-directed bullet wouldn't efficiently cure.

Villiers came into the latter category . . . when he'd been around.

Twenty-five years of age, the only alleged son of a property tycoon on the South Side, University drop-out, a drug dabbler with a severe dose of clap that had served to embellish his campaign medals in the Villiers war against society. Six feet in height, very fair, thin-faced, long-haired, bad teeth, something of a musician in that he had been able to play three kinds of stringed instrument; one didn't forget Villers readily. His form sheet indicated a case of car theft, one of assault, possessing cannabis and the like, and, lastly, murder.

The murder had been cleaned up, an open and shut job as the Press liked to say in their columns, to the entire satisfaction of the procurator fiscal. The officers concerned had been Sergeants James Collins and Stephen Pearson, M.M. The case had been closed just over three years before. Collins checked on the Villiers file for personal confirmation. Then he closed the file, placed it in a drawer of his desk and pressed a bell-button.

Twenty seconds later Albert Younger was ushered in by a uniformed constable carrying a notepad and pencil and shown to the chair on the other side of the inspector's desk. The constable went and sat on a chair near the door.

'Well, Mr. Younger, you asked to see me, I hear. Won't

you sit down?' Collins watched the young man's face as he spoke. A tidy client, this, with a pride in himself and, obviously, with a sufficient amount of cash to dress himself properly and with a degree of lavish indulgence.

'D'you mind if we – if we discussed this confidentially, sir?' Younger's voice was good, clear, articulate, baritone, oddly calm in view of his alleged purpose in that office.

Collins raised one forefinger. The constable stood up, opened the office door and let himself out without a comment being passed. 'Not at all, Mr. Younger. Haven't I seen you somewhere before?' Collins used this one on occasion. He had never seen Younger in his life, and was quite positive about that; so he opened the proceedings thus, and waited.

'Don't know if we have met, sir; but I know your brother quite well. We – we're occasionally involved businesswise.'

'I have two brothers, Mr. Younger. Which of the two?'

'Harry, sir. We meet on aeroplanes and trains at odd times.'

Aeroplanes, Collins reflected; the word was almost obsolete now. The class form was – aircraft, plane, jumbo-jet, chopper, VC 10, and the like. Here was a client talking about aeroplanes. Collins explored the cavity between his teeth with his tongue and sat back in his chair.

'Where d'you live, Mr. Younger?' Collins asked swiftly, watching the young man's face intently.

'Nine Greenfield Gardens, sir.'

Sometimes they were apt to give a snide address, trying to be sharp, or just plain cheeky with the duty sergeants. And promptly forget what they'd said. Younger wore a very heavy gold signet ring on the small finger of his right hand. It glinted dully in the reflected light of the neon tube overhead. Having answered the question with forthright honesty, he allowed himself to turn the ring upon the finger while he waited.

'Nice district, Mr. Younger. Like living out there?'

'I've always lived there, Inspector. With my parents. Yes, I like living out there – very much.'

'Ah. And I understand you wanted to talk to me about a

murder. Was that why you've come here? I ask the question because . . .'

'I came to confess to the murder of . . .'

'How long had you and Villiers known each other?' Collins broke in smoothly. Younger hadn't relaxed in any way, but he was ready to talk now.

'About a year, possibly a little longer than that. I actually met his father first of all . . . when I was working on a property development site that Mr. Villiers was promoting.'

'And Hugo came along in due course.' Collins nodded as he spoke. 'Fair enough. So you and Hugo teamed up; and then what?'

'Well, I was studying most of the time. I didn't run across him very often really . . . until that night.' Younger stopped and looked away.

'Take your time. I'm in no hurry, Mr. Younger. Just tell me what happened in your own way.'

Collins was expecting the old story about hitting the grass for the first time, but it had been drink. That tended to surprise him.

Younger and Villiers had been at some party. The festive season had been in full swing. Until then Younger hadn't experienced alcohol. Villiers had dared him. From there they'd gone on to another party. A few more drinks. A suggestion for a bit of a lark from Villiers. There was a warehouse he knew; a warehouse containing cases of whisky. A piece of cake to get in through the roof. Villiers had done it all before. Nothing to it. Nip in, a few bottles slipped out, and nip away again. Who would take any notice? The district was so full of drunks that the police had their hands full anyway.

What Younger was describing was making a whole lot of sense. It tallied with the details in the file this far. Collins let him continue. Younger wasn't rushing it like some of them did when they'd come to realize the door had closed on them. Younger simply stated facts. One could tell when the truth was coming across.

They had driven to the warehouse in the old van. Having looked the place over, Villiers had produced guns from under the driving seat. Guns, plural, Collins noted. They had found only one gun beside Villiers' corpse, a long-barrelled Olympic target job, registered officially as the property of the father of the deceased. Guns . . . plural . . .

Collins interrupted for the first time, quite gently: 'Mind telling me more about them, the guns?'

'Is that so important, sir?'

'I think so, Mr. Younger. Villiers produced these guns, and you protested immediately. Guns frightened you, and what they could do also frightened you. So you wanted to call it off. That's very sensible. I'm terrified of guns myself. Right, fair enough. You wanted to clear out there and then. But Villiers persisted that they were merely to serve as a possible deterrent. Now, just hold it right there. Let's have the description of the guns first.'

'One was this revolver; the one he gave me. The gun he had was a small-calibre target pistol, an automatic. He was quite a good shot, and there were silver cups in his house he'd won for . . .'

'The gun he gave you. Tell me about that one,' Collins steered him back on course gently.

'It was a revolver, an old one. Made in France, or Belgium, or somewhere. His father had taken it back from the war, I think.'

'Know the calibre of that one, do you?'

'Point three-eight. It was stamped on the barrel.'

'Ah. Three-eight.' Collins made a show of writing the detail on his blotter, high up near one corner.

No empty three-eight cases had been found on the locus. But then, of course, with a revolver the cases would have to be ejected manually. The only cases that had been found had been automatically ejected from the target pistol: all high-velocity .22-calibre rimfire brass cases. They had been proved against the pistol itself in the forensic lab. George Main had done that. Collins found his thoughts straying back to the Bolesco killing, with a seven-millimetre Japanese Nambu.

'How many shots did you fire, Mr. Younger?'

'Two. But when the night-watchman appeared round the corner, I did fire them in the air as Hugo told me. Well over his head. You see, one of them ricocheted off the wall and killed him,' Younger explained quickly. His voice had risen nearly an octave, and he was about to continue when Collins raised a hand for order.

'Steady! I told you there was no hurry. So you fired two shots. One ricocheted off – off what, Mr. Younger?'

'You don't believe me, do you?' Younger said in a strained voice.

'What gives you that idea?'

'You don't believe what I'm saying. You're treating all this as if it were of no importance. I can sense it.' Younger's voice rose again. 'You're just sitting there – not doing anything.'

'What did you expect me to do – rampage round this office and shout at you? This isn't the Army – this is a police office. I asked off what did the shot ricochet.'

'The wall, of course!'

'Which wall?'

'The wall behind him, I suppose. It was the only wall the shot could have struck . . . from where I was standing. Hugo had gone into the warehouse, you see. I never expected the man to come – I wanted to shout to Hugo but then I realized there was little point – I mean, if I'd shouted there would have been – he was there! Right beside me! I fired on the spur of the moment. Then I heard the echoes of the shots coming back off the walls – one after the other – crack, crack, crack – just like that.'

'What was the weather like at the time?' Collins asked evenly.

Younger's face twisted as the words conveyed meaning to him. 'The weather – you ask me about the weather when I'm trying to tell you I . . .'

68

'What was the weather like at the time you fired the two shots?' Collins stood up over Younger suddenly, a black ebony ruler slapping the top of his desk between them. 'What was the weather like?'

'Raining – sleeting – it'd been snowing. The warehouse yard was all slippery. When I turned to run away I fell on my face in the slush.'

'And the wind was blowing, too, I suppose,' Collins said loudly.

'I know you don't believe me now.'

'Villiers . . . did he come out of the warehouse when you fired those shots? Younger, I want to know where Villiers was at the time you . . .'

'I don't know where the devil he was. I fell on my face. The gun shot off ahead of me and I must have remembered to pick it up before I ran away. I swear I'm telling you the truth, sir!'

'But you heard the echoes of the shots, nevertheless. You're sure of that. Crack, crack, crack . . . right?'

'Yes, I've heard them every day and night for three years.'

Collins sat down. Younger had taken out a handkerchief and was mopping perspiration off his face, staring at the top of the desk, breathing with some effort.

Then Collins asked him: 'What do you do for a living, Mr. Younger?'

'I'm a sales executive, sir. I've worked very hard since that night. I suppose I tried to . . . I had to make some sort of effort to . . .'

'Sales executive. Which firm do you work for?'

'Ingerwell Electrics, sir,' Younger said in a whisper.

Collins pressed the bell-push and the uniformed constable answered. At a signal from his superior, the constable nodded and remained beside Younger while Collins took the Villiers file from his drawer and left the office. One of the waitresses from the café across the street was talking to Steve Pearson when he reached the charge room. Aware of his presence, the

69

sergeant and the girl both turned and looked in his direction.

'This is Maisie, sir,' Pearson explained unnecessarily. 'From over the way there – the café.'

' 'Evening, Maisie,' Collins said, giving her a brief smile. 'Trouble across the street, is there?'

'It's the young woman we've got in, Mr. Collins.'

Steve explained: 'Mr. Younger's friend, sir, far's as I can see. The lassie's been very upset.'

'She keeps on crying, Mr. Collins. I don't want to be interfering, and that, but I thought the least I could do for her was to come and . . .' The waitress shrugged as she broke off in conversation.

'I'm very grateful, Maisie.' Collins frowned in Pearson's direction for several seconds. 'I think,' he went on slowly, 'that you might go back and – no. Would you like to step into the waiting room for a couple of minutes, Maisie. Sergeant Pearson'll come and get you, and you can both go back and see what's worst with the girl. Just over there, Maisie.'

'Mind if I put a fag on, Mr. Collins, in there?' the waitress asked.

'Sergeant Pearson will let you have one of his.'

Steve Pearson obliged and lit the cigarette for the girl who moved into the waiting room and closed the door. 'What I like about you, Jumbo, is that you're a non-smoker. It makes life so much easier for you.'

'Not at this moment in time, mate,' Collins said. 'Younger was on that warehouse job with Villiers, Steve. I know he was, now.' He held up the file. 'Four and a half thousand words of report in here, and not a single syllable concerning Albert Younger.'

'And Albert Younger knocked off the watchman. Great – marvellous!' The duty sergeant pulled a face and stared down at the file. 'How the hell did we miss him if he was the . . .'

'He wasn't – Younger, I mean. Villiers shot the old man. But Younger reckons *he* shot him with a bullet that ricocheted off the wall. A three-eight-calibre shot, at that.'

'Where'd it go – up his rectal orifice?' Pearson suggested. 'Even if it had, the medical examiner and George Main would have known about it.'

'Try this one for size, Steve . . . Younger's a sales executive for Ingerwell Electrics.'

'Brother Rose's outfit! This world's full of bloody nuts!'

Collins neither agreed nor disagreed. He just stood quite still.

'How long have you been working for Ingerwell Electrics, Mr. Younger?' Collins asked the young man across the table from where he sat. The attendant constable had re-established himself on the chair by the door and was transcribing the interview word for word. Younger had agreed to his presence on Collins' suggestion regarding accuracy of the account as the procurator fiscal would require it.

'Almost two years, sir.'

'Doing what – precisely?'

'I went into the accounts department and, and the general manager discovered that I could speak French and German, you see.'

'Very good,' Collins said agreeably. 'More than I can say for myself. Even my English is on the ragged side. Go on, Mr. Younger.'

'Well, there was a board meeting came up, and this was disclosed and . . . well, they asked me if I'd be prepared to become an overseas representative. That's how I met your brother, sir.'

Collins nodded. There was no question about this young client. This was the real truth. 'Aha . . . right, on you go.'

'Well, sir, that has been the position since.'

'And all this has, very naturally, been preying on your mind; so you came to see me. Because you know my brother, perhaps?'

Younger nodded silently. 'There was another reason, Inspector. And that had a lot to do with it – two other reasons.

71

The first reason, the less important one, if you will forgive me, was because you have a reputation for fairness in the city.'

Collins grinned openly at him; his professional grin, but it usually managed to get through. 'Thank you, Mr. Younger. The other, *more* important reason now?'

'Because I want to marry someone, sir.'

'And that,' Collins said frankly, 'is the best reason in the world. Good for you.' He picked up the telephone and said: 'Steve, when you knock off, I'd like you to get a car and go down to the warehouse yard where we picked up Villiers. You look up for the impact marks of metal projectiles on the wall . . .' Collins paused and glanced at the young man.

Younger said: 'It would be the wall facing the entrance. Facing north, wouldn't it? Yes, north.' He nodded. 'That's right, sir.'

'The north wall, Steve. Take a couple of lads with you. I want to know if there are impact marks on that wall, how high, how far apart. Right? And have the lads run you home. I'll note your extra time. Fine.' Collins replaced the telephone slowly, asking casually: 'Don't you have a Mr. Rose on the board of your firm?'

'Yes, we do. I hardly know him, actually. He's what's known as a partially active director. Only appears at annual meetings, I think.'

'Ever spoken to Mr. Rose?'

'Never, sir. I did see him on two occasions, that's all.'

'His name came up somewhere or other,' Collins explained. 'A sort of association of ideas, names, you know how it happens.' He made a note. 'Had you ever fired a pistol before that evening?'

'No, sir. Never, ever.'

'And since?'

'No, sir.'

'Where's the pistol now, Mr. Younger?'

'I panicked and took the ferry to Belfast. The next day. I was born there. My aunt still lives there.' The words were emerging in sharp bursts, like verbal machine-gun fire. 'I stayed there for nearly three months. Read all the papers. And I . . .'

'And you . . . ?'

'I came back here. I had to. Never known why, exactly. I simply had to come back. I was on the point of coming here then. When I came back. But I didn't. I was in my final year, you see. I had to skip a full term at University as it was. I had to come back, that's all. That's all.' Younger's voice dropped to a mere whisper.

Collins said : 'That'll be all, Constable.'

'Usual procedure, sir,' the constable asked.

'Yes, get it typed and bring it back for Mr. Younger to read.'

The constable frowned and left the office. What was Jumbo on to with this lot? Part of the act, no doubt. It wasn't anything like a complete testimony. He was continuing to frown when he slipped the foolscap and carbon into his typewriter.

'Where is the pistol now?' Collins asked quietly.

'I chucked it over the rail of the ferry on the way to Belfast.'

'I see. And I think you said you heard three echoes.'

'There were three echoes, sir.'

'But you say you fired only two shots.'

'That is true. I fired two shots.'

'For three echoes,' Collins stated sharply.

'Echo from one wall to another,' Younger suggested nervously.

'Ah,' Collins said. 'Could be, I suppose. Would depend on where you were standing, in relation to the walls in question.' But he was happy about it now. He had read the report thoroughly. Three empty rim-fire cases had been recovered from the locus, indicating that Villiers had evidently fired three shots in all. Three echoes – that had been the quieter reports of the small-calibre gun from the roof of the warehouse. It all fitted. Had Villiers fired the third shot at Younger?

'What happens now, Inspector?'

'We put the matter through the appropriate channels, naturally.'

'And now you charge me with murder.'

'Why?' Collins asked him.

'Because I killed – I fail to understand what . . .'

'Mr. Younger, you didn't kill anybody. Hugo Villiers shot the watchman with two bullets from a competition rim-fire pistol of point two-two calibre. The case proved itself beyond any shadow of doubt. I don't begin to know what the procurator fiscal will decide to do about this.'

'So . . .' The young man sat in stricken silence.

Collins said: 'You might as well go home. Stay within immediate call for the next week. I may require you back here. Good night, Mr. Younger.'

He escorted the dumbfounded man out of the office, nodded clearance to the duty-men, and stood watching the silent departure.

The constable looked up from his typewriter, goggled, gaped at Collins, and waited.

Collins said: 'You can destroy it, Constable. I'll handle this one personally.'

'Very good, sir.' The constable removed the transcription from his machine, observed Collins' return to his office, and said to his neighbour: 'Maybe it's me who's daft.'

'No doubt about it. I've known all along.'

In his office Jumbo Collins sat at his desk and pondered.

The items of evidence were gradually mounting. Bolesco had been executed by three bullets from a Japanese Nambu automatic pistol of seven millimetre calibre. George Main of Forensic would return details of this rather rare handgun, perhaps by the time he came on duty the following day. The rarity of the weapon might resolve the case; on the other hand – who was to know? He lifted the telephone.

'Inspector Collins. Get me the Firearms Department.'

74

After a pause of several seconds, a voice said: 'Department of Firearms.'

'Inspector Collins. I'm looking for a Japanese pistol. A seven millimetre Nambu. It's rare. What have you got registered?'

The voice replied: 'It's rare, sir. Can you let me have a few minutes?'

'Of course. I'll wait. Check collectors, all collectors.'

But, of course, there was so little hope. This had to be a souvenir. This had to be unregistered. Bound to be.

Collins replaced the telephone and yawned.

Chick Harmon, Nat MacDowell . . . he could think of at least a dozen other names. It was like fishing for a sunbeam in a winter storm.

6

Somewhere along the river a ship's siren whooped twice in the thickening fog as Steve Pearson rang for admittance to the warehouse yard. A uniformed constable beside him flashed his torch through the tall bars of the entry gate. A light went on high on the wall above them.

'Who is it?' a hoarse voice demanded from an alley between the brick buildings.

'Police. Sergeant Pearson, North Division.'

'What's up now?' the same voice called irritably. 'I was just brewing a pot of tea. Always the same with you blokes.'

'Open up. We haven't had a brew either,' Steve Pearson replied.

'All right, I'm on my way.'

The watchman emerged with an inspection torch in his right hand, and a heavy pick shaft in his left. After beaming the policemen with the torch, then flashing it across to their car, he decided to unlock the iron gate.

'We just want to have a look round,' the sergeant explained.

'Who's lifted what this time?' the watchman asked in the same irritable tone.

'We'll write it out on a special report for you in the morning,' Pearson told him, slipping through the opened gate and his constable following. 'There's some flymen on the move round here.'

'I've just done a round. Never saw a soul. Been all over.'

'We'll go across this way,' the sergeant said.

'What about my brew in there?'

'We can manage, chum. Might drop in and have a cup with you on the way out. Sure, off you go and we'll look in later.'

'I'm supposed to accompany ...'

'Suit yourself,' Pearson said agreeably. He led the way down a narrow alley to where the loading yard opened out between the tall buildings. Two diesel trucks stood awaiting loading under ramp shoulders. The constable flashed his beam across them. Pearson thought back over the intervening three years. 'It was about here,' he muttered, looking about him. 'Aye, the old man – hmm. That's the side we want to look at then.'

'What you looking for, anyway?' the watchman demanded, lending the beam of his torch to those of the police. 'Better weather, or something, maybe?'

'We're always looking for better weather, chum,' Pearson said, his eyes following the beams. 'Hold it there.'

Three beams converged on a point. The sergeant produced a small pair of binoculars and focussed them with his right hand, then he examined the wall surface.

'That mark's always been there,' the watchman said. 'I know every brick on them walls. Every door and window and ventilator. Been looking at them for close on two years now.'

'Know any other marks like that?'

'Aye, up there, higher up.' His beam rose through several degrees and steadied on the point. The impact scar might have come out of the same mould as the first.

'Aye,' Pearson said eventually. 'We might send a couple of men along in the morning if necessary.'

'But what the hell for?' the watchman demanded.

'For something to do. We've all got time on our hands these days. Have to justify the taxpayer's money, you know.'

'I'll have to report this,' the watchman protested.

'So'll we too,' the constable said.

The kid brought in by the crew of Car M-Five was about twenty, black-haired, white, bespectacled, clean, tidy, well dressed; and very frightened. His name was Derek Spenser Quigley, his vocation was apprentice instrument maker.

The two patrolmen hustled him into the charge room where Charger Steed was typing a report. The time on the wall clock was eleven-ten.

The duty sergeant rose off his chair and listened to Constable Buchan giving him the strength on the pinch. It appeared that the kid had been driving a red mini erratically on Stenford Road. They had flagged him down and demanded where he was going. The kid was on his way home; and home was at the other end of Stenford Road, approximately eight hundred yards from the spot. They had asked him to blow up the bag. The kid had blown up the bag.

In the charge room Charger Steed examined the blown-up bag. There was no evidence of alcohol in the crystals.

'Did he make any objections when you asked him to blow it up?' the duty sergeant demanded briskly.

'No, not really,' Buchan said.

'Not really? Meaning what?'

'Well, he wanted to know . . .'

'I merely asked on what grounds . . .' Quigley began to say quietly.

'Shurrup, you!' Charger Steed roared at him.

Collins overheard the harsh vocal tone as he walked from the toilet back to his office. He turned and moved towards the end of the corridor, his head slightly to one side as he listened.

'May I have the use of a telephone?' Quigley asked directly.

'What for – ring up your bloody bird, I suppose,' Steed shouted.

'I'd like to contact my father's solicitor and . . .'

'You'll get no bloody solicitor here, lad.'

In the corridor, Collins let his tongue explore the cavity between his teeth. Charger was on top form. The old Army bull was boiling up beautifully. Collins waited for the kid to protest, but he chose to remain silent.

'What's your name?' Steed demanded sharply.

'Derek Spenser Quigley.'

'That what he told you, Buchan?'

Constable 'Book 'em' Buchan said: 'Right, Sergeant.'

'Any objections?' Steed asked the kid.

'I'd like to have some legal advice, please,' the kid said with quiet directness. 'This is the first time I've . . .'

'Nobody asked you for your bloody life story, lad.'

'In that case, I have nothing further to say,' the kid said.

'Oh, a smart bugger, are you?'

No reply.

In the corridor Collins frowned. He was thinking about the kid's name. Behind him, he heard his telephone ring, and went to answer the call, continuing to frown. As he closed his door he heard Steed bawling at the kid again.

'Inspector Collins, North Division.' He listened to the caller. 'Right. I'll send someone over there immediately. Just stay where you are, sir. Can I have your name again?' He wrote the name. 'And your address, sir?' He wrote the address quickly. 'Thank you, sir. There'll be a car with you inside three minutes.' He hung up, waited, dialled an inside number. 'Bill, get a crew and nip across to Woodfield Avenue – eighty-three. Snap it up. Break-in.'

'Right away, sir,' Bill Baker replied smartly.

Collins replaced the telephone and listened to the haranguing tones of the duty sergeant in the charge room. He was making the kid suffer. Collins sighed audibly, still frowning. It was not his province to interfere at this point.

Quigley stared directly at Charger Steed, standing very erect, not longer scared. The sergeant was giving himself away and his voice grew louder. As it grew louder so did Quigley's quiet confidence also grow. He answered quietly and in monosyllables, ignoring the hectoring oaths and insults.

'Are you going to sign this bloody form or aren't you, you smart bastard?'

'I'm signing nothing, nor am I a bastard,' Quigley quietly.

'Any more of that and I'll . . .'

'Sergeant – I don't know your name – but you're making me a bit sick,' Quigley said quietly.

'A bit sick. I'll make you bloody sick. Right, Buchan – and you, Thompson – get his stuff off him. Boots, tie, belt, braces. Turn out your pockets, lad!' Steed roared at the kid.

Quigley automatically folded his arms as the patrolmen advanced upon him. They had to force his arms apart in order to get into his inside pockets.

'Resisting officers of the law while in the execution of . . .'

'Don't be so ridiculous,' Quigley said quietly, in the same frank direct voice that had Steed blow up initially. He stood quite still and, as the patrolmen forced his arms apart, one of them stumbled and caught at the charge room counter for support.

'Kicking a police officer while . . .' Steed began to shout, his arm going out in a threatening gesture.

'I'm not in the habit of kicking people,' the kid replied sharply, 'not even policemen.'

His belongings were thrown on the counter in a pile. The sergeant came through the flap and caught him above the elbow, squeezing hard on the nerve. Quigley winced and tried to break free, to escape the searing pain in his arm.

'Going to make something of it, are you, you bastard?' Steed had his wrist in the other hand and was twisting it. 'I'll bloody well show you what's the drill in here.'

'Hadn't you better charge me first, Sergeant?' Quigley said through the pain and the indignity of it all.

'So you'd tell me my job – Christ, a right client you are!'

By then Inspector Collins was back in the corridor. He got into the charge room in time to see the kid being frog-marched towards the stairway that led to the cells. When the patrolmen and the kid had left the charge room, he said to the red-faced n.c.o.: 'Sergeant Steed.'

'Sir!'

'In my office, if you please.'

'Sir!'

Collins led the way to his office. The sergeant stood stiffly to attention while the inspector seated himself. Collins left him standing to attention. In a very level, quiet voice, he asked him: 'How long since you've held your promotion?'

'Four months ... sir.'

'Ah. I thought so. What concrete evidence have you got against Quigley, Sergeant Steed?'

'Evidence of Constables Buchan and Thompson ... sir.'

'And what's that?'

'Driving recklessly, resisting them while in the execution of their duties, and kicking Constable Buchan while being searched ... sir.'

'Pretty desperate sort of type – Quigley,' Collins said evenly.

'Like the rest of them ... sir.'

'Ah. Positive reaction in the breathalyser, was there?'

'I – haven't examined it properly yet,' Steed admitted.

'Reckon we ought to ask him for a blood sample?'

'Yes, sir.'

'I'll ring the medical examiner . . . if you think so.'

'Give us the confirmation we need, sir.'

'Again, Sergeant Steed, it mightn't. In fact, it might do precisely the opposite.'

'Sir?' Steed waited.

'What else did Quigley do?'

'Gave me a screed of cheek ... sir.'

'Did he call you a bastard, like you called him?'

'Well, he did ...'

'Answer my question, Sergeant. Did he call you a bastard?'

'No, sir.'

'Did he call the patrolmen bastards?'

'No, sir. But he refused to ...'

'Never mind what he refused to do. Have you arranged for a solicitor to offer legal advice to the kid?'

'Well, that is – no, sir.'

'Why not?' Collins snapped out.

'Well, I mean – I haven't had time, sir.'

'Picked up on – Stenford Road, wasn't he?'

'Yes, sir.'

'What time?'

'Eleven o'clock – twenty-three hundred, sir.'

'Ah. Know where Woodfield Avenue is, Sergeant?'

'I – no, don't think I do, sir.'

'Next thoroughfare to Stenford Road,' Collins informed him.

'Sir?'

'I know Quigley's case isn't exactly my province. But Woodfield Avenue is, as it so happens. Constable Buchan's known as "Book 'em", I believe. Right?'

'Yes, sir,' Steed answered swiftly, waiting, dubious.

'A zealous officer, therefore. Likes to have his book nicely busy, with piddling little items like picking up that kid down there. Because the kid may, or may not, have been driving erratically.'

'Got to keep an eye on them, sir.'

'But we don't necessarily have to call them bastards when they happen to be quite legitimate in every sense of the word.' Collins was barely whispering now.'

'I'm sorry, sir. Won't happen again.'

'I'm sorry, too, Sergeant Steed. I'm more than sorry.'

'Don't follow, sir.'

'Had Buchan and Thompson been, instead of hunting down kids in Stenford Road,' Collins said softly; 'had they been in Woodfield Avenue, they'd have, in all probability, caught the client who broke into number eighty-three . . . at approximately eleven o'clock tonight.'

'Wasn't aware of any break-in . . .'

'Of course not. Nor are Buchan and Thompson – because they choose to spend their time dive-bombing kids in mini cars whom they choose to imagine drive erratically to the danger of the general public. Right?'

'Well – yes, sir.'

'A great pity, Sergeant Steed,' Collins whispered. 'Particularly at this moment in time ... ah?'

'Yes, sir.'

'Also, a great pity they don't know young Quigley. I know him − I know all about him. Consequently I feel fairly convinced he was dive-bombed . . . because, for a start, he's recently passed the test for the Institute of Advanced Motorists − passed it with flying colours. He is also a total abstainer, like his father. And he is not a bastard, Sergeant Steed. I know that, too.'

'He was impudent, sir,' Steed replied, playing his only ace.

'Wouldn't you feel that way if I called you a bastard?'

'Yes, sir.'

'I trust you'll convey my sincere compliments to Buchan and Thompson, and inform them of the break-in at Woodfield Avenue. I also trust you will inform them that it would be to their mutual advantage if they were to bring that kid upstairs, return his property accordingly and permit him to go on his way. Whether they choose to offer apologies is entirely their own affair.'

'But, sir, it isn't as if they . . .'

'Know the name of the vice-chairman of the police committee, Sergeant Steed?'

'Well, well no, sir.'

'Obviously. I'll tell you. His name's the Very Reverend Andrew Knox Quigley, D.S.O., C.G.M., M.A., of the same same address. He also happens to be a particularly good and trusted friend of mine. A gentleman to whom I've gone with many problems.'

'I'm very sorry, sir,' Steed said awkwardly.

'You said that before. What else have you to say, Sergeant?'

'I − I'll see he's − I'll see he gets his belongings . . .'

'That boy's no more guilty of what you maintain than I am. We all make mistakes, even police officers make mistakes. But as a rule we make them unawaredly. You understand?' Collins whispered.

'Yes, sir. Naturally, sir,' Steed said through pale lips, his face like chalk.

'We don't make them deliberately,' Collins barked, 'like you three puddens have done tonight! If you've any complaints about that, see Superintendent Wishart in the morning! Now get out of my office – and try to behave like a policeman, and a responsible one. That's all.'

'Sir!' Steed executed an immaculate about turn, and marched out.

When he'd gone, Collins lifted his telephone. To the switchboard operator, he said: 'Inspector Collins here. Get me the number of the Very Reverend Andrew Knox Quigley, if you please ...'

And he tried to decide how he was going to explain to Andy Quigley the reasons for his son's apprehension.

Detective-Constable Dick Rimmer pondered at the bar of the Crystal Club. He had ordered himself a pint shandy, but at the Crystal Club they didn't carry anything as common as pint glasses; so he'd had to settle for a pale ale. The barman-bouncer who had carefully poured the drink had a form-sheet as long as his arm. Nothing desperately serious like arson, rape or murder, but a varied selection of just about everything else. Rimmer, like Collins at North Division, held a slight fixation that the Bolesco execution was essentially a domestic job. Nat MacDowell, Chick Harmon, Irish Pat . . . Irish Pat – a loner, a free-wheeling gelly man. Irish Pat was not known to concern himself with the mobs. And Bolesco had lifted him down the hill from the prison. Bolesco had stowed his loot away – somewhere. They all had their own ideas about hiding places. Some shoved it up the chimney, others put it into a numbered safe deposit, the clever men improved on all that.

Like with safes they had suitably lowered into ponds, or had cast into concrete floors. If the keys went missing, lost or stolen, or purposely chucked away; it would call for a gelly man to operate accordingly. And Bolesco had lifted Irish Pat that day.

The subject in question was seated with a busty redhead in one of the three alcoves Rimmer could see reflected in the mirror beyond the counter. Irish Pat was nicely fired by treble whiskies. They liked to live it up between terms inside. This kind of living cost money; more than they would normally have on liberation. So Bolesco had slipped Irish Pat some spending bread in the car on the way into town . . . and then some hatchetman had finished Big Tony.

Nat MacDowell and Chick Harmon. Chick had nearly bought it as well that morning, so with reluctance Rimmer cancelled Chick from the lists. That left Irish Pat and Fat Nat MacDowell, both of them Micks from Ulster. And Vincent Duffy, of late memory. He had been squashed into the deck a few days before Tony had been arrested. Vincent Duffy and Big Tony, both powerful men, could have handled the matter of the deposit-safe arrangements.

Of the remaining crowd in the club Rimmer failed to recognize only five. They might be anybodys or nobodys. One of them might be the contractor of that morning.

'How's the boy on a cold night like this now?' Fat Nat Mac-Dowell asked, clapping Rimmer on the shoulder. 'Put him up a real drink,' he told the barman. 'You can't be drinking cold stuff like beer in weather like this; now, can you?'

'I can just about drink anything anybody buys for me, Nat,' Rimmer admitted regretfully. 'I'll have a treble malt.'

'That's what I like to hear from a good friend,' MacDowell said, chuckling. He was five feet six in height, weighed around fifteen stone; and when he chuckled like this all of him rippled, belly, chins and small pudgy hands. His form-sheet at North Division was brief to the point of disbelief. A twenty-pound fine for careless driving. But he was the planner in the Bolesco mob.

All of which Rimmer considered as he said: 'Thanks, Nat. Bad luck on Big Tony this morning.'

Fat Nat spread his pudgy hands: 'In traffic like we have these days, it might happen to me tomorrow; or to you. Be reasonable. Nobody never lives for ever, Richard my boy.'

In the mirror Rimmer could see Irish Pat stroking the inside of the redhead's left thigh. Rimmer was considering his next move. The newspaper first issues would be on the street by this time. It was getting on for midnight. And two lines would read: 'The police are treating this as a case of murder'. Rimmer said: 'Who would want to knock off Tony, Nat?'

'What's that?'

In the mirror the surprise looked genuine, and it sounded genuine, Rimmer thought, as he said: 'You know Tony was knocked off, Nat.'

'Now I don't at all. What is this you're trying to tell me?'

It still looked, and sounded genuine. Fat Nat's hand was on his forearm, and the Mick was repeating himself all over again.

'Tony was shot at close range. Everyone knows about it. Even some of the passengers on that bus saw the shotholes. Come on, Nat, be your age.'

'I swear to the saints I didn't know a thing about it at all. What happened to Chick? We tried to get in to see . . .'

'You won't be seeing him for a long time,' Rimmer said. 'What's Chick done?'

'Doing – not done,' Rimmer replied. 'Withholding information. We can hold him on that for long enough.' He tasted the whisky thoughtfully. 'You know it is your civic duty to assist the police in matters . . .'

'Sure and I know that, Richard, but why in the world . . .'

'Chick doesn't seem to know,' Rimmer said wearily. 'So we hold him until he learns otherwise.'

'Then if you'll be after asking me what it is you want to know.'

'I did,' Rimmer said, almost convinced now that the paunchy Mick was genuine. 'Who'd want to knock off Tony Bolesco?'

'Nobody I'd ever met, Richard. This is terrible!'

'Right. You might be next. This client's a very smart number. It was all planned, beautifully planned. One day I'll tell you about it. In the meantime, think about it, Nat.'

'I must telephone,' the paunchy Mick said hastily. A fine gleam of perspiration had appeared round his chins, his eyes were unnaturally wide. All the signs pointed to sincerity and shock.

As he hurried away, Rimmer called: 'Thanks for the drink.'

But the Mick didn't reply. He just hurried out of sight through a door at the end of the bar, a handkerchief mopping his chins.

It still looked absolutely genuine, Rimmer thought bleakly.

And Fat Nat MacDowell was the planner in the Bolesco mob.

Detective-Constable Dick Rimmer finished his drink, stuck his hands deep into the pockets of his coat, and mooched out of the Crystal Club.

Detective-Constable Bill Baker got out of the car quickly as it drew up opposite eighty-three Woodfield Avenue. It was a small villa fronted by lawn that had been bisected with a double width path of concrete paving stones. The driver of the patrol car stopped his engine and pointed ahead to where an elderly man was appearing through a white-painted gate.

'That's probably the bloke, Bill.'

'Soon see. Good evening, sir. Are you the gentleman who reported the break-in?'

'Yes, I live next door,' the elderly man answered quickly. 'You see, I was walking my dog and there was this man came out of the lane at the side there and before I knew where ...'

'All right, sir. No hurry,' Baker said. 'Now then, you were walking your dog ... in which direction?'

'Up the road, that way. It's to the north, that way.'

'Where were you when the man appeared?'

'Just about ten yards or so behind your car.'

'And he appeared out of the lane.'

'It's only a narrow passage – a cul-de-sac actually. He barged out of the lane and knocked me over. I had to – I let go of the dog's lead, you see . . . and before I caught hold of it he'd run . . . away down yonder, towards the children's playground.'

'I see. That's very useful, sir. Could you describe him?'

The elderly man thought about it before answering. Baker approved of that. Witnesses, particularly after a knock, tended to rush the fences and exaggerate. He waited, watching the lined face and the Adam's Apple rising and falling as his informant swallowed.

'Well, he was rather tall. *Quite* tall. And he had long hair. Quite long hair. And it was fair hair. Quite fair hair.'

'Taller than me?' Baker encouraged him as he hesitated.

'Oh, taller than you are, I'd say.'

'Have a look down the lane first, lads,' Baker ordered. 'Take your time about it.'

'He broke the window, you know,' the informant said quickly. 'I . . . went and looked, you know. I suppose I ought to have . . .'

'You did very well indeed, sir. Can you tell me anything more about the man. Clothing, appearance, that sort of thing. Young or not so . . .'

'Oh, he was young. Quite young. Dark trousers . . . with wide – wider at the bottom of the legs than trousers generally ought to be.' The man swallowed again. 'I did notice his trousers particularly. You understand, when he knocked me over I fell and the way I fell, on my side, I could see him really quite well under the street light. Fair hair, long, tall. Ah, and his jacket had a belt.'

'Yes, sir. I thought that might be the case. Go on – this is all very useful information.'

'Anything the matter?' a voice asked beside them.

Baker turned to see a small woman with an umbrella. She must have materialized out of one of the lanes close by. No one had been on Woodfield Avenue when they'd pulled up.

'Everything's in order, madam, thank you,' Baker said pleasantly. 'D'you live on this street, by any chance?'

'No, I live on Stenford Road. I take the short cut, you see.'

'I see, yes. And you've just come from there?'

'Yes, of course. There *is* something the matter, isn't there?'

'Nothing that ought to concern you, madam. Good evening.'

The woman walked on slowly, looking back at intervals.

'She's the district nurse, sir,' the elderly man whispered. 'Likes to know what's going on, and that.'

'Notice anything else about the man who knocked you over?'

'Can't think of anything else,' the man replied after thinking for several seconds. 'The Barretts are off on holiday; gone to Italy. They have a daughter living out there. On the embassy, the daughter is. In Rome. I have a look over the place occasionally. They're very nice people.'

'D'you have a key for the house?'

'Oh, yes. Got it here with my own. I check on the heating at the weekends for them – and on Wednesdays.'

A constable came out of the lane. 'Diamond job, Bill. He had the paper in operation as well. Want to have a look?'

'I'm coming. Put in a call for the team.'

'May I come, too?' the elderly man asked. 'I've never seen a burglary.'

'Better if *we* have a look round first, sir. If you go back home, I'll come and see you in a few minutes. You've been very helpful indeed so far. I'll borrow the key for a moment, please.'

'I hope you get that – that young bugger.'

'We'll certainly try, sir.'

Baker accompanied the constable to the locus. The second policeman drew their attention to the broken window. 'Blood. See that – double-glazing. He didn't reckon with that, I guess. Blood's on the inside pane of glass.'

Baker weighed it up carefully. 'Probably cut himself on the

outside pane and it dribbled down between the two as he was working on the second pane. See the way the drop's fallen? Yes,' he muttered thoughtfully, 'it's going to be helpful, that droplet.' He flashed a torch along the wall of the villa, and then moved round to the front door which he opened with the borrowed key.

Baker surveyed the room with the lights on. It was the lounge of the villa. Furniture was thrown into a heap, covered with items of clothing. Cupboards had been opened, their contents strewn on the floor. Drawers yawned open from a bureau, bottom drawer pulled out first and lying on the floor. Some client with a form sheet. In the alcove at the front window stood an oval mahogany table, highly polished on top and with delicately carved ornate legs. A smashed china vase lay underneath the table, along with several artificial flowers and a circle of napery on which the vase had stood. The top of the table had been heavily gouged with parallel lines in the form of crosses. The jemmy that had produced this infamy had been smashed repeatedly into the pattern of crosses.

'A pattern there,' the patrol driver observed thoughtfully.

'Useful pattern,' Baker replied. He wasn't really seeing the appalling scars. He was seeing faces; faces that belonged to tall young louts. He was also mentally tabulating a short leet of the names of some of those tall young louts.

The lights of a car swathed the window glass as the vehicle pulled up outside the house. The driver said: 'That's the team now.'

'Okay.' Baker nodded absently, and turned to see two of the arrivals enter the room. They wore khaki overall coats and carried heavy leather satchels. They didn't talk. Only their eyes worked. With the merest of nods to Baker, they produced the tools of their trade from the satchels and proceeded to search. Baker told the driver: 'You come with me. Willie can go back with them.' To one of the arrivals he said: 'Here's the house key,' and tossed it into the man's right hand. 'We're going looking for a client.'

'Who're we looking for, Bill?' the driver asked as they drove down the quiet street.

'A client with a bandaged hand. Who's taller than we are? Who's got long fair hair? Who's a diamond scratcher?' Baker asked, and there was confidence in his tone of voice.

'I can think of three for a start. No bother at all.'

'That's right. We'll look them up first. Out to Loch Road.'

'That's Knocker Jarvis. He was one of my three.'

'Who else?' Baker replied.

'Littleton and Potter,' the driver answered promptly.

'Right both times. Let's go.'

The patrol car swept down Woodfield Avenue ten minutes after midnight.

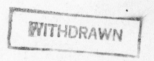

7

Robert Tullo Whitehead and Harold Potter were brought into the charge room within five minutes of each other. Whitehead had a form sheet that included car theft, assault and fraud. He was thirty years of age, white, five feet eight inches in height, weighed 160 pounds, had the words Hate and Love tattooed on the back of the fingers of his right and left hand respectively, wore his hair cropped, and had no fixed address. When he'd been picked up he'd been dossing in a derelict church.

Bill Baker formally carried out the usual procedure in the presence of duty sergeant Steed and the driver of the patrol car. A uniformed man brought in two brand-new carpets, their price tags still attached, and placed them across the charge room counter. He stood awaiting orders.

Baker said: 'It's on the late side to have the evidence identified. Take him downstairs.'

Whitehead protested: 'Hey, what kind of set-up's this? Youse lot's never found anything on me. I've never seen them carpets . . .'

'Where did you get them, Bill?' the duty sergeant asked Baker in a bored voice.

'They were in the old organ loft. ' Baker's voice was equally bored. 'You've no imagination, have you, Bobbie?'

'Hey, there's other five sleeping in the old church. Why'd'youse have to pick me out? That's what I want to know. It's a bloody liberty, so it is. I've never stole anything in my life.'

'Except a Ford Consul, you mean,' Baker told him.

'I just took a lend of the car!'

'And it got you free board for six months, that's right.' Baker frowned at him. 'And now you've taken a loan of these carpets. That's going to get you more free board, about eighteen months of it, I'd say. Okay, away with him.'

They took Whitehead downstairs, still protesting his innocence. Baker had some small degree of respect for some of the clients. The clever ones, that was. Like Chick Harmon and even Fat Nat MacDowell. Because they were clever, and that was all. For the Whiteheads and the like there was nothing but disgust. Because they were so incredibly stupid. And they never learned.

'Bring in Harold Potter,' he said to the uniformed men. 'I think we'll have his form sheet, Sergeant, if you please.'

'It's right here,' Steed said, producing the file, and stood in silence while the detective scanned the offences.

Except for one conviction for assault, Potter's form was a straightforward record of breaking and entering. The system never varied. Potter never used a car. He persisted in wearing a belted jacket into which he stuffed what he stole. He persisted in using a diamond glass-cutter. No less than two of Potter's tools were in the production room. Both were of the same make, size and colour. Baker dropped another of precisely the same on the counter. The duty sergeant found a label and affixed it to the glass-cutter. Baker nodded and signed the label, dating it and giving the precise time.

Collins appeared from his office and surrendered the file concerning the late but unlamented Hugo Villiers. 'I'm going home, Bill. See you tomorrow afternoon.' He glanced at the labelled production on the counter. 'Potter again?'

'Yes, sir. They're bringing him up now.'

'Good night, all,' Jumbo Collins said and went out to get his car, wondering what the hell to do about Albert Younger. There was always Frank Wishart to consult, of course. Passing the buck, maybe. Then it would be up to the P.F.

Potter was brought in for charging. He was six feet two in

height, weighed 178 pounds, blond, long haired, and when apprehended had been wearing the familiar belted jacket, bell-bottomed black trousers, and a soiled handkerchief had been tied round his left wrist. Eleven years earlier he had been convicted for breaking and entering at the tender age of sixteen. The driver of the patrol car placed a plastic bag on the counter. It was labelled and signed accordingly by Baker.

'Get that filthy bandage off, Potter,' Baker said quietly.

'What for?' The voice was sullen.

'Because, mistakenly no doubt, I'm concerned for your health,' Baker said. 'Let's have the first aid box, Sergeant Steed, if you please.'

'I'm not taking it off!' Potter shouted.

'Better if we let him die,' the driver said hopefully. 'Blood poisoning's just as effective as anything; except that it takes a bit longer.' The driver was watching Baker's eyes. Baker winked his left eye. The driver pounced. Potter struggled with him. But they got the soiled handkerchief off his wrist very quickly. A narrow, clean hairline wound was still bleeding slightly. 'Cut yourself shaving, I suppose,' Baker murmured.

'Aye, sure; that's right,' Potter agreed almost perkily.

'Bring him down the passage,' Baker told the uniformed men.

They escorted Potter into a room where five tall men were waiting. All five were approximately the same age as Potter, two of them were plainclothes constables, and the other three had been asked to co-operate from the streets outside.

'Just in case you've forgotten the drill, Potter, you may stand beside any . . .'

'I remember the drill, sure. But if you and them other . . .'

'Shut up, Potter,' Baker said quietly. 'You'll be told when you can talk. Right, Sergeant Steed, bring in the witness, please.'

The elderly man who'd been knocked down by a blond, long-haired running man was ushered into the room. He had been instructed what to do beforehand. He walked along

94

the line-up, looking directly at the tall men, walked back along the line and, after some deliberation and scrutiny, pointed at Potter. He didn't say anything, and the duty sergeant ushered him out. Baker thanked the members of the line-up and waited until they'd left the room.

When the last had departed, he said: 'You can carry on, Sergeant Steed. Make arrangements for his and Whitehead's appearance in the morning. I'll confirm that in writing now. One copy to Superintendent Wishart, as usual.'

'Right away,' Steed said and, turning to Potter, roared at him: 'What you waiting for – move!'

Potter moved – downstairs.

Baker watched them go, disgustedly: wrote his confirmation.

The time was one-fifty a.m.

Time to go home. Baker read what he had written, yawning.

Baker went home.

Detective-Constable Dick Rimmer slouched into North Division two hours and eighteen minutes after midnight. He ignored the muttered greeting from the duty-men behind the charge room counter, and made his way to the general C.I.D. office. Dusty Miller and a D.C. called MacInnes were studying the men on a miniature chessboard. Mugs of steaming cocoa stood on either side of the board. MacInnes was humming a Hebridean love-song. He was of a fair complexion, ruddy cheeked, with a badly broken nose, and his eyes were so incredibly black that it wasn't really true. Something, Rimmer morosely reflected, that had to do with a possible Armada bloodstreak in his breeding over the years.

MacInnes spoke English with the perfection of the natural Uist-man. He also spoke his natural Gaelic, and was a gold medallist for poetry and song. He was thirty-one years of age, and possibly the most dangerous man with his mitts in North Division. He also had a devious mind. At that moment he betrayed this latter facet in his next move across the chess-board. Dusty Miller put on a rueful face and brushed his chess-men flat before returning them to their little box.

Miller asked Rimmer the expected question about the Bolesco execution, and shrugged off the negative reply. 'It'll come through in its own time, Dicky,' he said with a cheerful-ness he didn't feel.

'I got a line on that hoist of stuff from the Excise ware-house, though,' Rimmer told them quietly.

MacInnes scratched the side of his neck below his collar. 'A sample of that would be worth something at the moment. It was nearly all proof strength, according to the complaint. Do we know where it might be, Dick?'

'In the lock-ups down on Braid Street,' Rimmer said. 'I've got it covered for the time being.' He was more concerned with the initial reactions of Fat Nat MacDowell. The bonded spirits were safe enough, now that the stake-out was in action. The moment the clients came to collect, the job would be sewn up conclusively. Rimmer wondered if he'd been pru-dent to hit MacDowell with the news as he had. The moment the word had spread that Bolesco had been killed had brought in the usual flow of nuts anxious to confess to the job. But Fat Nat had . . . had *seemed* to be quite genuine. He said to MacInnes: 'Hamish, how about you having a look about?'

'That is what I get paid for,' the Hebridean said agreeably. 'What would it be that you want me to look for, Dick?'

'The movements of Nat MacDowell from – well, say the past forty-eight hours.'

'Alibi time, likely,' MacInnes suggested. 'Aye, likely.'

'You might say that. It's a point that hadn't entirely escaped my notice.' Rimmer's voice was sour. 'I'm going to write up the Braid Street information, and then I'm going to get my head down in the locker-room for the rest of the night. I'm dirt done.'

'Whatever you say.' MacInnes glanced at his chess partner. 'Are you on for this as well, Dusty?'

'Better'n sitting here. I think I know where to start.'

'Two heads are better than the one,' MacInnes observed, as he slipped on his coat and a cloth cap, 'even if one cannot play chess worth a . . .'

'We can't all be bloody brilliant,' Rimmer interrupted sourly. 'For which, may the Blessed Lord be sincerely thanked.'

'Amen to that,' MacInnes said heavily; and, raising his head in thought, quoted: ' "Let them be confounded that persecute me, but let not me be confounded: let them be dismayed, but let not me be dismayed . . !" '

'I can't compete,' Rimmer shouted, and departed to find a typewriter.

Dusty Miller and MacInnes slipped out by the rear entrance, got into a small and rather battered saloon car, and quietly drove it out from the car park behind North Division.

MacInnes was humming another Hebridean lullaby, and very beautifully.

Inspector Jumbo Collins woke with the uneasy dawnlight beginning to filter into the bedroom. His wife slept on. Rita had always been a placid girl and a regular and deep sleeper. They were both glad about that. Without disturbing her, he crept out of bed, tucked the disturbed bedclothes about her, covering her back, and went to dress himself and shave before brewing their habitual morning cup of tea. He wasn't concerned about eating anything yet. Rita would rise in her own time and begin the day's routine.

Sparing a moment to peer down at their young son in his cot, he moved into the bathroom and ran the hot tap, finding one of the open razors and stropping it thoughtfully before heating the blade in a tall jar. He had the ability to close off that part of his mind concerned with the more trivial matters of professional life, and to concentrate on the major items. The two in particular at that moment were Albert Younger, and the late Tony Bolesco.

He was continuing to concentrate on them when Rita woke and called gently to him. He soaked his smoothed face in hot water, and then in cold and, rubbing his cheeks with the tips of his fingers in a sharp massage, went back to the bedroom and bent over the bed to kiss her. Collins still managed to derive as much enjoyment from this as he had done on their honeymoon. God had something to do with that – God had a lot to do with everything, Collins believed.

'I didn't hear you come home, Jimmy,' Rita said sleepily.

'Good,' he said to her softly, both of them listening for the first whimper from the child in his cot. 'I was out with another woman.'

'What was this one like?' Rita chuckled softly as she asked the question. 'Nice? Young? Coloured?'

'She was white, about forty-twenty-eight-forty-two, brunette, very wealthy, runs a B.M.W. 2500, has a house at Glen Denny, a cottage in the Trossachs . . .'

'That's quite enough for me to be going on with, Jimmy.'

'And she has a beard,' Collins finished, kissing her again.

'Ummm.'

'And we're going off to have a dirty weekend . . .'

'Ummm!' Rita interrupted.

'Next month,' Collins continued.

'Then I can take the baby down to Mum's for a day or two.'

'Ah. Might be an idea,' he agreed thoughfully.

'Are you going to tell me about it, Jimmy?'

'I have told you, chicken. Cottage in the Trossachs . . .'

'About Tony Bolesco,' she persisted.

'Maybe tonight, tomorrow – next day. Depends.'

'Isn't there anything at all for you?'

'Very little. I'll get the brew going. You stay here.'

'I'll get up, Jimmy.'

'No need. The boy's still asleep.'

'You'll have to eat some . . .'

'Later. I'll get a plate of something in the canteen later. I want to get up to the hospital to talk to Chick Harmon.'

'Will they allow you, at this time of the morning?'

'Aha. They'll allow me. I have a special passport.'

'Pig,' she said. 'Remind me to go off you some time.'

'If I remember,' Collins whispered to her and, with confident fondness, cut off any verbal riposte she may have chosen to make.

Rita emitted a sound like: 'Hmmmm!'

Collins went out of the room to attend to the first brew of the day. There was no call to involve Rita with Albert Younger. Damn Albert Younger. But Albert Younger was still there, about twelve inches in front of his eyes. Write him off as another of the nuts who came to confess? It was hardly fair to go and dump the show in Frank Wishart's lap at this stage. According to the book, Albert Younger ought to have been booked and some charge or other concocted that would hold him in custody for further investigation. . . . And Steve Pearson had confirmed the shot scars on the brick wall of the warehouse . . . but how the devil was one to prove, beyond all shadow of doubt, that Albert Younger had ever been near the place where they'd found the bodies of Villiers and the watchman? The whole set up was as crazy as a warped nightmare.

He could hear the interview with the procurator fiscal . . .

'*And you decided to inform Younger that the watchman was killed by Villers, Inspector? Why?*'

'*Because that was the form of the case, sir. The truth.*'

'*But why?*' *The P.F. had a brittle, dry, severe voice.*

'*Because Younger would have discovered the truth in any case, sir.*'

'*I hardly follow your reasoning, Inspector Collins,*' *the P.F. would inevitably reply in that dry voice, a trifle sarcastic.*

'*With respect, sir,*' he might begin to explain – again, he might not decide to explain anything regarding his actions. Hell, he had enough to do with the nuts, the Benjie Booths, and the like, and the Bolesco execution had been very smart indeed; very crisp; very well planned and executed. This wasn't the work of any kind of nut. This had been absolutely immaculate; perfectly timed, notably sinister. What the devil did it matter if Albert Younger had been told to go home with his girl? Did the P.F. expect him to put *her* downstairs as well, to comfort Younger in the green-walled cell, so that they could spend the rest of the night indulging themselves in the digestion of the list of conditions and regulations posted on the wall for the edification of newcomers to official hospitality?

His reflections were abruptly terminated by one of the cups being knocked over to fall with an almost musical vibration of fractured destruction on the tiled floor. Collins breathed an involuntary oath very sharply.

'I heard that, Jimmy,' Rita said behind him.

The baby whimpered in his cot.

'Sorry, chicken.' He seldom if ever swore in her presence.

'I'll go through to him,' she said softly. 'If you want to talk about it, Jimmy. That's why I'm here. I might be able to . . .'

'There isn't enough. Not nearly enough – yet.'

'But it could escalate into . . .'

'It could. Tony Bolesco was important enough. Let's leave it for the moment. I'll try and get home for lunch. I'll ring by half-ten. Okay? Bill Baker and Rimmer can work on it. Who knows; they may have got it all sewn up already.'

'Optimist,' she said as she went in to see the boy in the cot.

But Collins didn't feel very optimistic when he went into the special ward where Chick Harmon was being shaved by a white-coated male orderly. The orderly was a middle-aged man with a composed expression. His real name was Peter Culbard. His real rank was Detective-Sergeant. Chick Harmon merely knew him as Redford, like every other member of the hospital staff below the rank of medical-superintendent. A uniformed man was seated near the bed, and he stood up to attention when Collins entered. Collins waved to him to be seated, wishing him the time of the morning as was his habit with the lower ranks. Good manners didn't cost a farthing;

but they often produced some degree of honest respect and co-operation.

Harmon's colour was slightly better. Collins glanced at the record card that hung from the lower bed rail. Temperature looked steady. He didn't waste too much time on the card. He nodded to Harmon and waited until Redford had finished the work of tidying-up. Before his formal entry to the special ward, Collins had spent several minutes in the ward orderly's office, reading a note left for his attention in a particular cupboard. The report had stated that Nat MacDowell had visited the establishment the previous evening, on two occasions; and had also telephoned in that morning to inquire about the patient's progress. MacDowell had not succeeded in any one of these manoeuvres.

It also stated the names of the duty-men who had been in attendance throughout the previous day and night. A short professional summary on the patient's progress and present condition terminated the neatly written note. Collins had pocketed the note, thinking about how long Redford, or Peter Culbard had been a detective-sergeant.

'Breakfast will be served in fifteen minutes, sir,' Redford informed Collins. 'May I bring you a cup of tea, or coffee and biscuits?'

'That's very kind of you,' Collins answered formally. 'I don't think this will take very long.'

'Very good, sir,' Redford said quietly, gathering his bowl and shaving equipment, and left the special ward.

'How's it going, Chick?' Collins asked the patient.

'I've got a headache, and it's got worse over the last two minutes. What'd'youse want now?'

'You and Tony lifted Irish Pat yesterday morning. Why?'

'Just taking him down the road. I told you that yesterday. Why go harping on about it all?'

'Because I want to find out who shot Tony, for a start. For a second card, I want to know where the loot went.'

Harmon eased himself higher in the hospital bed with an

effort. The dressing had been changed across the upper part of his face, but it was of such a fashion that Collins couldn't watch the man's eyes properly. 'Look, Jumbo, I don't know what happened to the loot. I wasn't even around at the time. I was down in the Smoke. You know that; it's all written down in the . . .'

'Down in the Smoke so's not to be about the manor when Vincent Duffy got his – right?'

'All right, all right. We both know I didn't like Vincent Duffy. He was knocking off my bird – right. So I didn't like him at all. But I never touched the dirty little Irish bastard. Honest to Jesus, Jumbo – I had nothing to do with that.'

Collins was inclined to believe it. Duffy had been liquidated by Bolesco himself: something like an electric impulse in his mind had always made him believe it had happened like that. Duffy and Bolesco had hidden the loot, and then Duffy had died, rather horribly; under the wheels of a heavy-duty truck. No one knew where the truck was, either; no one ever would, now, because Bolesco had had his.

'What was the form with Irish Pat, Chick?' Collins asked evenly.

'No form. We just gave him a lift down the road. You know what Tony was like – was a great guy; kind to his parents, and that.'

'I know what Tony was like, Chick. I know how long I can hold you, too. And I'm holding you to the full extent . . .'

'But what the hell have I done? I nearly got it myself!' Harmon touched the dressing across the upper part of his face.

'One hundred and ten days, Chick,' Collins reminded him. 'And it won't be in here. Beds are in short supply. You'll go up the hill and into "K" Wing.'

'I can't believe you'd do that, Jumbo. I know the kind of reputation you've got – you're reckoned to be a fair-minded man.'

'What did Tony and Irish Pat talk about on the way down?'

102

'Sex . . .'

'You told me that yesterday. What else?'

'All right. It can't do Tony any harm now. Irish Pat was to meet him at his place at eleven o'clock – hey, that's today.'

'Go on, Chick.'

'That's it!'

'Go on, Chick. You've given yourself away – by a mile. Go on!'

'Tony said for Pat to take kit with him for about a week.'

'They were going out of town somewhere,' Collins said.

'Sounded like that to me, aye.'

'Why?'

'I . . . don't . . . know. Now, that's the truth, Jumbo. I don't know.'

'But you'd be driving them, right?'

'Maybe. There was nothing passed between Tony'n me about that – you could be right. Maybe he might've wanted me to drive. But he never said as much. Never got the chance; did he?'

Collins turned and went to stare down on to the street outside. This sounded like the real thing now; but he couldn't be certain. The form was to tell some of the truth and no more. Sometimes this worked; sometimes it didn't.

Still staring down at the street, Collins asked: 'Where'd Nat MacDowell figure in all this?'

'Nowhere. How could he? Nat's in Dublin.'

'Ah? Doing what?'

'Giving away his niece. The kid's getting – she got married yesterday.'

'In Dublin?' Collins checked.

'In the Church of Our Saviour on Liffey Drive.'

'That's interesting,' Collins murmured slowly. There was a reason for this.

In the ward orderly's office, Redford picked up the telephone and rang in to North Divison, giving details and what was immediately required. Presently, after he'd replaced the instrument on his bracket, Collins' voice said: 'So Nat's in Dublin, is he?' And Redford resumed the transcription of the interview being transmitted through the small speaker on the desk beside him.

'Nat's been in Dublin since Monday,' Harmon explained. 'The lassie happens to be the only youngster he's got. His sister's kid. She's a right wee smasher, too.'

'When's he due to come back, Chick?'

'You can search me on that one, Jumbo. Last time he went across, he was there for a month.'

If this one checked out, Collins reflected, it might cancel the possibility of a domestic liquidation. Down on the street below, he recognized a retired inspector of police with whom he'd worked on his first assignments. The tall man marched well, held himself erect, and had stopped to talk to a middle-aged woman outside a newsagent's stall. Three years had elapsed since the retiral. Now the ex-inspector had a security job with one of the light engineering concerns near the river. Collins mentally wished him luck: he owed him a great deal.

Turning back towards the patient, he asked: 'This can't do Tony any harm now either, Chick...'

'Honest, Jumbo, I don't know a bloody thing about the stuff.'

'We'll scrub round that lot, for the moment. I'm trying to find the client who shot him. You held him in high regard. Right, be a bit sensible. Let's both work on this – the client who shot him. Right?'

'I'm right with you,' Harmon said instantly.

'Since Tony went up the hill,' Collins asked evenly; 'who's been taking care of Joy Sinclair?'

Harmon reached up to ease the dressing on his head, pressing it sufficiently far up that his eyes became visible. Looking directly at the burly man cast in hard shadow by the light of the window, he said: 'Now I follow. Makes a lot of sense, too. Some geezer knocking off Joy. I'll have to think about it, Jumbo.'

'I've got plenty of time,' Collins said.

Redford appeared with a tray. 'Breakfast, Mr. Harmon.'

Collins caught the eye of the uniformed duty-man. 'You can fall out and have something, if you'd like to. Mathieson, isn't it?'

The uniformed man stood up smartly, nodding: 'Yes, sir. Thank you very much, sir . . . if – if it's all right with . . .'

'I'll send the orderly for you when I'm ready to go, Mathieson.'

'Thank you, sir,' the constable repeated, leaving the special ward.

'Sure you won't have a cup of tea, Inspector?' Redford offered.

'I'll be glad to. Thank you . . . ah . . .'

'Redford, sir.'

'Thank you, Mr. Redford.'

When the orderly had gone for the offering, Harmon said: 'I could have sworn Redford was one of your zombies, Jumbo.'

'The public purse won't rise to policemen playing nursemaid in hospital wards, Chick. Sometimes I only wish it would, though. An idea worth thinking about. They could sit around and listen to clients like you talking in their sleep.'

'You should be on at the Empire, so you should.' Harmon began to tackle the steamed fish, sampling a bit of crisp toast.

'Let's get back to Joy Sinclair, Chick. Come on, come on, we've both got kindred interests in this case now. I'll get round to the loot later on, and I don't think I'll be worrying you about it. Who was looking after Joy Sinclair's domestic interests?'

'She . . . used to go up – no, hang on; that's two/three years back now.'

'That'll do for a start. Where'd she go up to?'

'Some place up the Strath Garry direction. I can't remember – Strath Garry . . . and there was a geezer who used to appear at the Crystal Club . . . he only appeared about a couple of times, like – then we didn't see him again. But I kind of got the notion that he and Joy were – well, you know what I mean.'

'Know him again?' Collins pressed.

'I'm not that sure that I would. It was a good while back now. I think he was real well stacked with ready. Good suits, and that, you know. Fancy gold wrist-watch. I mind on the watch.' Harmon paused and dug the spoon into a marmalade jar. 'But he never came back, see?'

It was the first time Collins had seen anyone eating steamed haddock along with marmaladed toast. The sight tended to knock him off the trend of events. At that moment Redford appeared with a cup and saucer and several circular biscuits. Collins thanked him and waited until he'd returned to his office. Then he said: 'I'm going to make a deal with you, Chick. I'm not overly fond of you, or of any of your mob – which is natural. But we both want the answer to this killing. You have two whole days in which to think, and to think damned hard. I want to know everything there is to know about Tony's opposition, his birds, his business deals . . . yes, fair enough, you can be as discreet as you like; and you'll know exactly just how far you can go. Work on it, and work hard on it.'

'A deal, you said, Jumbo. You've only given me orders so far.'

'You give me a lead to follow up, and I'll have you out of here the moment the medical superintendent pronounces you fit to move. There's your deal.'

'It's either that or the full stretch up in "K" Wing, like.' Harmon was spreading more marmalade with difficulty on another piece of toast. 'You're on, Jumbo. When you coming back in?'

'All you need to do is tell the duty-man – that's all. He'll have his orders. And while I'm at it, our people found the fourth bullet. It was embedded in the side pillar of your car. It went in there after it scratched you.'

'Scratched!' Harmon's voice sounded distinctly hurt.

'That was all it did. You were lucky, Chick. But you'll have to go carefully, for all that. This client meant to have you, too. That means you also get down to thinking about all the louts who bear you a grudge. Must be loads of them, too. Your name was on the gate with Tony's. It's my duty to inform you of the fact.'

'Thanks. Thanks a million,' Harmon muttered.

'No need,' Collins said harshly. 'So very unfortunately it's also my duty to afford some measure of protection to the public. You happen to be one of them.' The burly detective sipped some tea and put the biscuits into his pocket absently. 'Let's get back to this client with the expensive clothes and the gold watch; come on!'

'I'd tell you if I could remember, Jumbo,' Harmon protested. 'I'd be a bloody fool not to, wouldn't I?'

'That's the intelligent attitude now. How tall, fat, thin, dark, fair, colour of eyes, colour of skin . . . think, Chick!'

'I can't see the bastard anywhere,' Harmon said weakly.

'Strath Garry then. Get into Strath Garry. Have you ever been up there?'

'No. It's a name on the map to me, that's all.' Harmon pressed fingers against the dressing above his eyes. 'She could tell you herself; Joy, like.'

Collins smiled thinly. 'You're miraculous. What're you trying to do – act the goat with me?'

Harmon shook his head. 'I see the point. Hey, when you get a belt like this, you don't get too good about thinking.'

Collins nodded. That was fair enough. Impact, pain, shock, suspended reaction . . . and possibly a fair shot of sedative to keep the patient from crying himself to death. 'All right. I'm going now. Settle down and try and concentrate on this mug.' Collins called for the orderly. When Redford appeared, he asked:

'Would you call up the duty constable, Mr. Redford, if you please? I'm leaving now.'

'Right away, sir.' Redford disappeared.

Harmon chewed moodily on the toast. Then he said doubt-fully: 'I did notice something about him, but I'm beat to remember what it was.'

'His voice,' Collins said sharply. 'How'd he speak?'

'I just don't remember, Jumbo,' Harmon admitted after taking several seconds to consider that question. 'Not a word.'

Collins tried another tack. 'If you want to see your legal representative, I'll relay the information accordingly, and promptly.'

Harmon's bandaged head shook slowly as he chewed. 'Can't see what good anything like that would do me now. Thanks all the same.'

'Nat MacDowell tried to contact you.'

'I don't want to see Nat. I don't think I want to see any-body.'

'Where'll you go if I decide to . . .'

'I don't know that either.'

That makes two of us, Collins reflected. The duty-man en-tered the ward and stood until Collins made a move to leave. The orderly began to tidy Harmon's bed, and took the empty fish plate away. Collins grunted a valedictory mumble, and followed the man out of the ward, his face blank, his tongue exploring the gap in his teeth.

In the orderly's office, Redford silently handed him a note.

Thanking him, Collins read that the inquiry into Mac-Dowell's trip to Eire was affirmative; that the man had re-turned off the late plane the previous night; that a wedding had taken place at the Church of Our Saviour in Dublin the previous day at precisely twelve noon.

Collins stared directly at Detective-Sergeant Peter Culbard and thought about it. Culbard returned the stare.

'You reckon Fat Nat directed the job, Pete?'

Culbard shook his head. 'He's too fly for anything like that.

Nat's sharp; but he's as windy as hell about violence. We both know that, Jumbo.'

'Directed, I said,' Collins reminded the sergeant.

'Even so – no, I doubt it.'

'Me, too,' Collins admitted and walked down the corridor to where two young nurses awaited the arrival of the lift.

8

Sergeant Steve Pearson was on duty in the charge room when Bill Baker arrived at North Division to start another day's working stint. The detective accepted the sheaf of reports and appended his signature on a recept form, wishing Pearson the time of day and taking the papers to his own office adjoining that of Inspector Collins. Policewoman Sheila 'Slim' Summerville was pecking at the keys of the typewriter in one corner, looking distinctly weary and dejected.

'Morning, Slim,' Baker greeted her, glancing over her shoulder as the words appeared on her report. 'So that's where you've been all night.'

'Um.' Slim's head nodded slightly while she typed on.

'Alone?'

'Umhum. And bored to tears. I knocked off about three and went home. Only just come in.'

She had spent four hours at the Round Square Club in Blantyre Avenue, dancing with various casual and temporary acquaintances, had succeeded in fending off two amorous clients who had offered her money for the pleasure of her horizontal company in their flats, had been obliged momentarily to injure a third who had tried to use force for the same purpose, and had eventually been driven home by her colleague and fiancé, Dusty Miller, who had appeared shortly before three a.m., having completed the assignment with Hamish MacInnes on the recent movements of Nat MacDowell.

She had no evidence on the passing of dangerous drugs at the Round Square Club. No evidence whatsoever. Nevertheless, the report had to be written, copied and filed accordingly.

'How's your own horrid sordid world, Bill?' she asked, yawning again and excusing herself delicately.

'One day nearer the grave,' Baker said morosely. He was reading the first report, from Firearms Department, on the query regarding a seven millimetre Nambu automatic pistol of Japanese manufacture. No such firearm was officially registered, either at North, South, Central or County. 'Well, that's going to mean something, or nothing,' he said.

'What, Bill?'

'The gun we believe killed Bolesco.'

'What kind of gun?'

'Japanese Nambu pistol . . . according to George Main at Forensic. George's doing a double check on the bullets.'

'Interesting,' the attractive girl observed, tossing a cigarette on to Baker's desk and lighting another for herself. 'Ugh – first fag's always a bit off after a night on the tiles.'

'You ought to stop it, Slim.'

'Smoking, or going out on the tiles?'

'Both – except when it's vitally necessary. How – interesting?'

'Japanese gun. Could have been Bolesco's own.'

Baker laid the report down slowly. Looking across in her direction, he frowned. 'Like to go on from there?'

'He could have brought it home from the war. I know this is all topsy-turvy, Bill. The way my mind works. Association of ideas, facts, or whatever. Japanese gun, Japanese war.'

'One does tend to lead to the other. Where do they both lead?' Baker continued to frown at her. 'We're working on the assumption that, if it does turn out to be as George Main suspects, the client who hit Bolesco brought the pistol home as a souvenir.'

'Which is exactly what I said. Bolesco could have brought it . . .'

'You mean he was involved in the Jap fighting?'

Slim nodded. 'Didn't you know that?'

'I'm just a young policeman, sweetie. No, I didn't know.

How d'you know he was out there?'

'I read a Parole Board report somewhere or other. Steve'll have it. I'll go and see if he can . . .'

'When did you read the P.B. report?'

'Must have been three or four weeks back. Tony seems to have been quite a soldier. He got a decoration for . . . for bringing some sort of patrol out of a Japanese ambush, somewhere in Burma, or Malaya. I'll go and find it for you.' She got up to go.

Baker said: 'Three or four weeks back I was on leave.'

'So you were. D'you want to see it?'

'Thanks, yes. Bolesco's war record might still be with the Ministry of Defence, or wherever the military types keep their case histories. Can we put something together on having a copy of that – soon?'

'Leave it all to auntie, Bill.'

'Would Jumbo know about that report?' Baker asked quickly.

'Probably not. Jumbo's got more to do than read funny little compassionate P.B. remarks.'

Baker absently lit the cigarette she'd tossed to him. He was staring at a series of photostats of the suspected weapon. They had been copied from a standard work on the firearms of the world's military forces, the information stretching back more than two hundred years. A scribbled note from George Main had been clipped to the sheets. Baker glanced at it, and then at the photostats; but he wasn't really seeing them . . . if Bolesco *had* brought back a Nambu souvenir, someone in his mob may have known about it; and been aware of its rarity: and appropriated it for the single purpose to which . . .

Bill Baker was continuing to fit the parts together when Collins joined him in the office. The inspector had spent the previous half-hour upstairs in Frank Wishart's sanctum, discussing the case of Albert Younger. There was so little they could do in that direction regarding any kind of conviction. There was no proof except for the impact marks on the warehouse wall, and, of course, Younger's voluntary admission. To present a case of this nature would be the uttermost folly. The Press would give it a great deal of treatment. Younger and his girl would suffer abominably. The young man might even lose the job he appeared to be doing so well. All of which Frank Wishart had been at pains to point out; all of which Collins had found acceptable and reasonable. Now it would be up to the P.F.

Collins felt neither relieved about that, nor did he feel anxious. It was like a tide at full flow; like a bird hovering and awaiting the next thermal to afford it more lift. He grunted the time of day to Baker and went to scan the correspondence awaiting his attention.

Only when Slim Summerville returned with the copy of the Parole Board report did Collins look up, glancing first at the girl's face, then at the document she brought.

'Morning, Slim,' he said. 'What's this?'

'P.B. remarks on Bolesco, sir.'

'How edifying,' Collins grunted and returned to his correspondence. Seconds later, he asked: 'Why the interest?'

'Slim came up with the suggestion that – if Forensic are right about the type of gun, sir – it may have been a souvenir brought back by Bolesco from the Japanese fighting in Burma,' Baker explained.

'Go on, Slim,' Collins murmured, nodding.

'It was only a suggestion, sir,' the girl said. 'I happened to find this in the file, and . . . and I got the impression . . .'

'Let me have a look at that, if you please,' Collins said, holding out his right hand. 'I'd forgotten Tony was out there – maybe I didn't know about it. He got himself a gong for something or other; I do remember something about that. So he was up against the Japs.' He devoted the next minute to the P.B. report in silence. Eventually, returning the report to her, he said: 'Ah – aha.' His tongue explored the cavity between his teeth, his face going momentarily lopsided. 'So one of the mob knew about it, got hold of the gun . . . ah.'

Baker's eyes moved from the direction of the inspector, and then to that of the attractive girl. They both waited. But Collins had resumed interest in his correspondence. Even when the telephone on Baker's desk bleeped the burly inspector paid no attention.

Baker lifted the instrument and said: 'C.I.D., D.C. Baker.' As he listened, his pencil jotted down shorthand symbols on a pad. His eyes found those of Slim Summerville, held them, then swivelled in the direction of the door. The girl picked up the P.B. report and let herself out of the office. Collins began to pay attention. 'Yes, I've got that.' Baker spoke formally, his pen working swiftly. 'I see. Yes, you ought to know. I don't doubt what you say. Right – thanks a lot. I'll send someone down to square you this afternoon. Cheers.'

Collins said: 'Tip off, Bill.'

'Yes, sir.' Baker named his informant, and said: 'Nel Abney's in the manor, sir.'

Collins' face went lopsided. He said: 'Ah.'

Nelson Rodney Blake Abney, English, white, about thirty-four or five by now . . . Collins pondered upon the client. As a member of one of the London mobs, he'd shot a police informant to death but a jury hadn't been convinced of his guilt and he'd walked out of court. Abney had been twenty years of age at the time. Three years later he'd been convicted of fradulent dealing and had pulled down two years in Wakefield. But a few months after release from that establishment, Abney had been charged with murder, convicted, and some crackpot psychiartrist had saved him from the long drop. The murder had been that of a prostitute, and Abney had used a gun on that occasion, too. They'd sent him down for life. This time a Parole Board had wept upon each others' shoulders and decided he was a reformed little man who would be perfectly all right now.

And Abney was in the City. And Abney was known to be rather a clever client with a handgun; one of the very few.

Collins asked: 'Where was he seen, Bill?'

'According to the information, he's lodging in a house in Ruby Street, number sixty-six.'

'Doing what – for a living?'

'No information on that, sir.'

'I can imagine,' Collins retorted.

'The owner of the house,' Baker said, 'is Nat MacDowell.'

'Ask Steve Pearson to bring in his . . .' Collins paused. 'Do we hold that file here, Bill?'

'If we don't, we can get it, sir.'

'Right,' Collins said quickly. 'We want a copy of the form sheet, set of photographs, full physical description, the lot – get them out to all patrols – *all* patrols. I want to know what Abney does, where he goes, to whom he talks, and . . .'

Knuckles rapped on the door.

Collins called: 'Enter – whether he spends freely.' Glancing at the little man with the dissipated face, he said: 'Morning, Pixie.'

Pixie Greer nodded at Baker, and said: 'Morning, sir. I got the word you wanted me back.'

Collins paused for reflection. 'What's the griff on the Round Square midden, Bill?'

'Slim's report's in your in tray, sir. Nothing doing, apparently. She was down there last night, and this morning.'

The small thin man who would have passed for a professional jockey stood waiting beside Baker's desk. Greer had a personal disapproval of girls operating amongst the dregs of society at dumps like the Round Square. Dangerous drugs, and the occasionally dangerous clients who dealt in them were his own bucket of bother; and he was, and knew it, the expert in the field. But even experts didn't argue with Jumbo Collins; not for very long, anyway. Pixie Greer waited silently.

Collins said: 'Ah,' but didn't bother to consult the Slim Summerville report. Instead, he grunted: 'Get Abney's form sheet, Bill. I've got a small job you might work on, Pixie. Know Braid Street?'

'Yes, sir, quite well.' Greer's voice was soft and deep.

'There's a yard with vehicle lock-ups,' Collins observed, with Rimmer's report in his hands. 'Okay?'

'I know the yard, sir.'

'Without wishing to be too instructive, I want to know in which of those lock-ups one would find numerous cases of hoisted booze. I also want to know who comes to collect them, and when. There's a stake-out in operation. Steve Pearson'll let you know who's on it. It's all yours. Dick Rimmer's been dossing in the locker-room. Okay?'

'Yes, sir. I'll collect my tools on the way out.'

'That's it, Pixie. We're on the appropriate wavelength.'

Greer smiled thinly, nodded, and went in search of Detective-Constable Dick Rimmer.

Just before the hour of noon that same day, Detective-Constable Hamish MacInnes pulled a red VW Variant saloon into a lay-by overlooking the small village of Strath Garry, produced a pair of binoculars from a case, focussed them carefully, and spent the next two minutes making a slow, detailed and accurate survey of the settlement some six hundred yards down the valley from his vantage point. He hummed a Hebridean love lilt softly as the glasses swept from one establishment to the next. The village – it was no more than that – lined each side of a second-class road. On an eminence behind the older buildings, a small block of local authority houses were under construction; raw, ugly erections of pale grey concrete and pale pink tiled roofs, screaming against the placidity of the mellowed sandstone of the older buildings. The pattern was the same throughout the country. Even in his native islands the wind of architectural change had blown over the decades.

He mentally recorded the scene; the hotel, the post office and general store, a contractor's yard, a chemist's shop over the door of which was suspended the traditional, gilt finished pestle and mortar . . . MacInnes approved of the pestle and

mortar ... the local garage with its backyard filled with derelict vehicles ranging from a large lorry to a trio of rusting
motor-cycles, the garishly painted transport café in whose
front court stood a brace of articulated container trucks and
three family saloons with roof-racks bearing skis and camp-
ing equipment, possibly on their way north to the Avie-
more Centre where the first of the winter snows had been
reported a week previously. A group of children were engaged in some project in their school playground.

Still humming quietly, he cased the binoculars, checked
his watch that the hour of noon had arrived, and lit his
first meditative cigarette of the day. Tobacco and the dram,
MacInnes was convinced, should not be indulged until the
sun was at its zenith. He checked the contents of the VW,
the tourist's portmanteau, the anorak, climbing boots, sleeping bag, and a selection of large-scale maps, all intact and
obvious. The car bore a German registration, was left-hand
drive, and displayed the Deutschland nationality plate.

And the hour of noon had arrived and passed. Hamish
MacInnes started the engine and took a bearing on the hotel.

The girl behind the counter of the lounge bar was buxom,
very attractive, and her hair could have been naturally
auburn. She wore no jewellery except a small necklace that
was a simple silver cross. The young Hebridean noted the
silver cross and switched on to the appropriate wavelength,
as Jumbo Collins occasionally liked to quote.

At his side of the counter sat a middle-aged couple discussing food prices. MacInnes nodded to them pleasantly, ordered himself a dram and a half-pint of beer, lit his second
cigarette of the day, and casually surveyed the selection of
whisky on the shelves behind the attractive barmaid.

Eventually he asked the girl: 'Could you tell me where the
chapel might be, miss?' He asked the question in a deliberate
native accent. 'I couldn't see it as I drove in.'

The girl didn't hesitate. 'You wouldn't, from the road. It's
back off the road in the trees behind the school.'

'That would explain it. I came up from the south. It's quite a wonderful day for the time of the year, isn't it?

'It's not bad.' The girl was aware of the battered nose, the incredibly dark eyes and the sweep of blond hair. 'Did you want to see Father Martin?'

'Well, I did, yes. I'm trying to trace a relation of mine who used to live here, you see. Well now, I'm not too sure that she did, but she wrote me a couple of postcards from here once.'

'You from the outer islands?' the girl asked tentatively.

'Originally, I was. I've . . . been abroad for a while; in the Army, over in Germany.' MacInnes was aware that the middle-aged couple were paying attention.

'Father Martin would likely know about her, then,' the girl said.

'I was hoping that he might. I'm on my way north to do a bit of climbing, so I thought I'd try to find Joy if she's still in the district, you see.'

'Joy?' the male member of the couple asked quickly.

MacInnes nodded pleasantly at the couple. 'Joy, yes; Joy Sinclair. Hang on . . .' He produced a wallet and some papers and selected a monochrome photograph. '. . . This is her. Taken about six or seven years ago, of course.' He extended the snap for the man's perusal.

'I was thinking about Joy Spence. She's the wife of one of one of the local farmers.'

MacInnes said: 'She might be at that. I've been out of . . .'

'Not the same lady,' the man said, showing the photograph to his wife. The woman shook her head while her husband said: 'She's not unlike you, is she?' Looking again at the image, he inquired: 'Your sister, perhaps?'

'My cousin,' MacInnes said pleasantly. He was watching the barmaid as the image was passed across to her. 'Recognize her, miss?'

'No, I . . . don t think I do. I've only been here two months.'

The girl added helpfully: 'But Father Martin's almost bound to.'

'Where you from, sir?' the man asked.

'The island of South Uist. Haven't been there for ten years.'

'Army, eh? Commissioned?'

The detective-constable shook his head. 'Sergeant, sir. In the Sappers.'

'All very different from my time,' the man said gloomily. And with a note of pride he offered: 'Scots Guards.'

MacInnes had already noted the navy and red tie, and nodded, replacing the photograph in his wallet. 'I was brigaded with them for a bit. Well, I suppose I better not waste too much time. Thank you all very much. He tossed down the half-pint of beer and bid them farewell pleasantly, walking out of the bar, able to hear the man observe: 'Good type, that chap. Tidy; good bearing.'

MacInnes began to hum another Hebridean lilt, feeling slightly better. Compliments didn't come his way every hour of the day.

Outside in the front court, a couple of children were playing a game of Tig, racing round the cars, one trying to catch the other; school satchels hanging low down their backs. MacInnes stood, his eyes on the children, and decided to try the garage next.

The staff at the garage hadn't seen the girl in the photograph, either. The gilt mortar and pestle gleamed from above the door of the chemist's shop almost directly across the street. The Joy Sinclairs of the world bought the merchandise of such establishments. He left the VW in the garage forecourt and crossed the street.

An elderly man wearing a spotlessly white overall jacket and gold-rimmed half-moon spectacles peered above their frames at him as he surveyed the trim of the shop. MacInnes didn't waste time.

'I'm sorry to bother you, sir, but I was wondering if you could help me to find a cousin of mine who used to . . .'

In faultless Gaelic, the elderly man answered: 'Certainly I will, if it is my power to do so. Where are you from?'

MacInnes began to feel that this might be his day. He said, in the same tongue: 'The island of South Uist. Daliburgh.'

'I was born at Ardivachar.' The elderly man smiled at him. 'And a good few years before Daliburgh ever found you, boy. Did you know the MacDonalds of Pollachar? A great piping family.'

MacInnes nodded immediately. 'I take a bit blow at the pipes myself.'

The shrewd old eyes held MacInnes' own. Presently they puckered in a flash of amusement. 'And you'd be looking for your cousin. A female cousin, likely as not?'

'Aye, a female cousin. I've been in Germany for a while, you see. I'm going to the Cairn Gorm to climb. I'm on leave, and I thought I might have a look for her.'

'Surely, surely,' the old chemist agreed, his head nodding.

They were considering their next cautious move when a young man entered the shop, glanced at MacInnes tentatively, licked his lips and nodded to the chemist. 'Morning, Mr. MacLean.'

'Another fine day, Alan. You'll . . . be wanting another roll of film, likely?'

'A film – another roll of film.' The young man nodded jerkily in return and glanced towards MacInnes again. 'Nice day,' he offered hesitantly while the old man disappeared temporarily into the depths of his stocks.

'Not bad for the time of year,' MacInnes said evenly, aware of the other's somewhat tense condition. The laddie didn't look like a junkie; but one had to make allowances. 'Local, are you?'

'Oh yes, I was born in Strath Garry. I work at the butcher's shop, and that. Serving my time, you know.'

MacInnes nodded. 'Wouldn't fancy it myself.'

'Och, it's all right; and the money's reasonable.'

'Now then, Alan, there you are,' the old chemist said from

his side of the counter. He passed a sealed package envelope across to the young man. MacInnes glanced at it: it might have contained a host of possibilities: it wasn't quite large enough comfortably to contain a conventional roll of film, though. 'That'll be fifty pence,' the old man said.

The young man paid and collected the small package, wished them the state of the day and left the shop.

MacInnes turned to see the old man's eyes puckering into a full faced smile again. The chemist explained: 'They're a bit shy about asking for French letters if a stranger's present.'

The detective constable found himself echoing the smile. 'I'm shy myself, Mr. MacLean. Still a fair trade, eh?'

'Oh surely. The pill knocked a bit off the bottom of the market for a while, but I began to take in the exotics, and that settled it back again.'

'Exotics, you said?' MacInnes asked doubtfully. It struck him at the time that the subject of the present conversation hardly merited the term used.

'Oh, very. Very exotic. You can get them in four colours, you know. Sea-green, sky-blue, bright red . . . and black. Twelve pence a time; fifty for five.'

'Black? You said black?' MacInnes said.

'Handy for funeral days, you might say.' Mr. MacLean grinned, but his eyes remained shrewd. 'Aye, aye, so you're home from Germany and you look like a MacInnes from Ard Ruairidh; and fine I know that both the sons of Angus Archie MacInnes went to the police, and not the Army. What does this cousin of your own look like?'

MacInnes failed to conceal his astonishment, and produced the photograph of Joy Sinclair.

The old man accepted it and studied it first over the top of his half-moon lenses and then through them. 'Umhum. Aye, aye.'

'Recognise her?'

'I've seen her about the place. Not for a long time, though. Not for a long time.'

'How long – any idea?'

The old man laid down the photograph and was drumming on his counter with all fingertips. After several seconds of this, he turned and left MacInnes to his own devices. MacInnes pocketed the picture and waited, his uneasy mind dwelling on the shock factor of an anxious maiden when confronted with a black one for the first time. The sudden reality of a sea-green specimen might be even worse. But it was good to know that a new slant in domestic humour had been propagated for the benefit of the world's young lovers. MacInnes felt quite happy about that. He began to hum a Hebridean love song softly as he waited for Mr. MacLean to return.

He returned to the counter with a leather bound ledger measuring some eight inches by ten. Embossed on the front cover ran the legend: poison register. MacInnes maintained a straight face: one never knew what an old joker like this might produce next. A chorus row of black rubber contraceptives danced somewhere in the air between his eyes and the book.

'When you get a special customer in this trade you don't always mind on the name, you know,' Mr. Maclean explained. 'You mind better if it was adiposis delorosa, nephritis, colic, Dehli boil, cellulitis, goitre, or trophoneurosis. In this particular case it was simple bronchitis.'

MacInnes nodded bleakly. 'I see what you mean . . . I think.'

'So that automatically led me to ephedrine.'

'I see,' MacInnes repeated.

'And in those days a patient had to sign this register. They've tightenened up on that since – all this drug affair and so on – and a patient can only get ephedrine on a prescription now.' Mr. MacLean leafed through the rectangular pages of his register. 'Four years – maybe less; maybe more. Are you in a terrible hurry, MacInnes?'

'I'm the elder one – Hamish, Mr. MacLean.'

'Hamish . . aye. You own brother would be Calum Archie.'

MacInnes nodded silently. He knew more about the family than Hamish did himself. 'That's right, as sure as death, Mr. MacLean.'

'Fine I know that, *gille*.' The old fingers leafed through the book.

MacInnes waited, humming another lilt melodiously.

Eventually Mr. MacLean found the applicable page. 'Aye, here it is. Bronchitis . . . Mrs. – can't make it out if it's Mrs. or Miss. Does it matter, Hamish?'

'Not a bit,' MacInnes answered patiently. 'Not a bit.' He was waiting for the name of Joy Sinclair to emerge in the audible sense. But the old chemist announced a quite different name. The name meant precisely nothing to the young detective constable. Nothing whatsoever. All the clients had their own choice of aliases. That didn't matter a bit, either. One was eternally prepared for that.

'Would that be right, Hamish?

'Aye – maybe more than right.'

'Is that a fact now?' Mr. MacLean expressed open satisfaction.

'It is that – a fact. It is that, and no mistake at all.'

'Well, well, now. Would you believe a thing like that now?'

'We have to believe anything in the trade.' MacInnes made a show of taking notes in his official book, writing in beautiful small copperplate script; openly, on the smooth counter, while the old chemist watched the movements of the pen.

'Do you always write like that, Hamish MacInnes?'

'It is what I was taught at the school at Daliburgh,' MacInnes said.

'Man,' the chemist said regretfully, 'I'm thinking the local two doctors would have been better educated in the same place.

'And why, Mr. Maclean?' MacInnes asked with interest.

'Their prescriptions – the forms, you know – sometimes

I have half to stand on my head to make them out. No hen scratching across a midden ever did as bad. Oh, aye, and by the way, she used to live up at the house yonder. Come you across here to the window and I'll point it out to you. It's called – The Spruces. Up there – and you can see the big spruce trees as well. The owner's a big man of business down in the city.'

'Aye, aye,' MacInnes eventually observed with the confusing profundity of the true Hebridean. 'Well, well, now that's a thing, and no mistake.'

'Aye, and so it is,' Mr. MacLean also observed with the same uncanny profundity.

9

Two dungareed males drove a dilapidated Ford Escort into the muddy yard fronting the vehicle lock-ups on Braid Street. One was tall, thin, gangling to a degree, and appeared to have a permanent sour facial expression under the ragged cloth cap he wore. The other was short, stocky, rotund even, looked like a drop-out from a drug den, and wore turned-down wellington boots and white stockings, into which had been tucked the dungaree trouser hems.

They drove the car into the yard, partially reversed the vehicle, so that it stopped within a yard of the nearest lock-up doors, and sat in apparent deep thought while their eyes and ears sized up the local situation. Two minutes later, the short man emerged from the car, looked about him once more, and went to work on the nearest padlocked door with a selection of bent and twisted wires he carried suspended from a steel ring. The taller man behind the wheel lit a cigarette and apportioned his immediate attention on the entry to the yard. Beyond the entry, across the adjacent street, a young couple were comfortably established in a Wolseley 1800, arms about each other – there was no shame in the world now, even at the hour of eleven hundred – and directly upon this young couple Dick Rimmer concentrated his unbelieving gaze. He knew, of course, that the couple were Dusty Miller and Slim Summerville. Snogging, Rimmer reflected, was all very well – and his own snogging days had long since passed – but when you could go out snogging in the middle of the day, and *get paid* for it . . . that was planning!

Rimmer glanced across the lock-up yard. His companion had disappeared. One of the lock-ups' double doors were slightly ajar.

Presently the smaller man emerged and, with a quick twist of one of the bent wires on the steel ring, he relocked the padlock, shaking his head in Rimmer's direction. Then, after a glance around the yard, he went to work on the door of the next lock-up. Rimmer, in the car, leaned back in his seat and yawned.

Inside the lock-up Pixie Greer flashed a small torch beam across the interior. The place was a shambles of disorder for, in place of the expected vehicle, furniture of all shapes and descriptions had been piled haphazardly, some of the items carelessly covered with dirty dust covers. A number of plywood tea-chests were closest to the doors, each container bearing a tacked-on inventory of the contents. Greer carefully prised one of the inventories free of its case and unfolded the sheet of paper and read the listed items . . . picture frames, vases, crockery, bowls, and an electric frying pan.

The investigator was prepared to believe it, and reattached the inventory to the case. After another cursory survey of the interior, he backed to the doors, listened, caught Rimmer's nod from the waiting car, slipped outside and relocked the doors. The entire operation had occupied less than three minutes; but it had been quite thorough.

Eight minutes and three other lock-ups later, Greer discovered what he was looking for. The interior was about three-quarters full, the cases of potable spirits neatly packed in orderly fashion and thus affording speed of recovery and transportation. He let himself out of the lock-up and went back to the car.

'It's here, Dick. What's your form?'

Rimmer scowled in the direction of the courting couple in the Wolseley beyond the entry. He spat through his window and gave the matter a little consideration. 'You get back in there. I'll get Slim organized to clear the stake-out and Dusty can lock us both inside. Better take the rations with you.' He passed a small case of liquid and solid nourishment to the little man as he spoke.

'I can fix that – the lock. It's a spring padlock. No bother from the inside. Let's be having that cabinet screwdriver, so we can ease off the door hinges at one side. Might pay later on.' Greer winked at Rimmer as the sour-faced detective gave him the tool. 'Cheer up, neighbour; we might get a medal each for this one.'

Rimmer spat through his window again and said: 'Bollocks.'

But Greer paid no attention: he was on his way back to the lock-up.

Rimmer was watching the couple in the Wolseley as he prepared to speak into a miniature walkie-talkie unit. The girl disentangled herself and went through the motions of arranging her hair. Rimmer was unable to see what her consort was doing, but he knew, nevertheless.

He said into the mouthpiece: 'Dee to Dee, over.'

Dusty Miller's voice replied: 'Receiving, over.'

'It's all here. We're in operation. Collect our car when you're ready. Give me a signal if the street's clear, over.'

'Okay on all that,' Dusty Miller's voice stated. 'Stay on the given frequency. I'm clearing the other lads, but I'll stay with you until relieved, over.'

Rimmer nodded at the instrument, thinking about the drill. 'Aye, fine.' The 'other lads' were at that moment investigating a suspected coal-gas leak somewhere along the street; hammering a steel spike into the surface and testing gas with a meter placed across the spiked holes. Another 'lad' was taking care of the window cleaning for any interested householder on Braid Street. 'Leave Robbie at his windows,' he said after a while, 'just in case, over.'

'Right, I agree. I'll clear the gas mob now, over.'

Rimmer watched Slim Summerville getting out of the

Wolseley, pausing to glance up and down the street, and then pick her handbag out of the car. As she proceeded to come in his direction, Rimmer nipped out of the Ford Escort, and joined Pixie Greer in the lock-up. As Greer brought the doors together and began to work on the padlock, Rimmer spoke again : 'We're in position, over.'

'Good luck. Check transmission on the hour, over.'

'Yes, sir. Very good, sir, and Good morning, sir. Out.'

Rimmer switched off the unit before Dusty got an opportunity to think up a verbal riposte. He and Greer listened to the Escort's engine being started, and the battered old car being driven out of the yard.

'Now,' Greer said in his deep and oddly soft voice, 'we wait.'

'I've been waiting all my bloody life,' Rimmer replied sourly.

Hamish MacInnes studied the approach to the Spruces before deciding upon future action. The house was massive, and would have been cubically ugly had it not been partially covered with ivy and surrounded by a well kept lawn dotted with flowering shrub and ornamental bushes. The drive was immaculate, the small shingle surface recently raked and the edges of the lawn neatly trimmed. A regular implantation of granite boulders had been arranged, with military precision, to act as a guard for the grass against the inroads of carelessly driven vehicles. MacInnes noticed all these things with approval.

The window frames and sills had been recently painted. The rather old-fashioned heavy brass door handles and knocker were brilliantly polished. On the west side of the house a lean-to conservatory's glass was catching the sunlight, reminding him of an enormous precious gemstone. Each of the house windows had been opened exactly two inches from the top; each curtain arrangement was precisely the same as its neighbour.

MacInnes frowned and endeavoured to plan his approach

to the obviously scrupulous occupier. Only after several minutes of concentrated reflection did he cautiously drive the VW up the slope to the Spruces.

He was given no chance to get near the front door. Before he could get out of the car, a voice demanded from a ground floor window : 'Are you the television engineer?'

MacInnes was aware of a pair of hands on a sill, and the vague shape of somebody within the room beyond. He made his best smile of the day and replied: 'I'm sorry, no. I was wondering if I might have permission to . . .'

'I'll be out. Just wait,' the voice said instructively, and the hands, leaving their resting place on the sill, closed the lower frame of the window.

MacInnes got out of the car and straightened up his collar and tie. He felt rather thankful that the VW was reasonably clean for once. The owner of the voice turned out to be a middle-aged woman, very tall, impressive, almost severe in countenance. She might have been a duchess, for all he knew. She certainly looked like one, MacInnes felt.

'Good morning, madam,' he said pleasantly. 'My name is MacInnes. I wondered if I might have permission to camp for the night on your grounds.'

The woman's eyes widened visibly. 'At this time of year? Camp? In a tent, you mean?'

'Yes, madam.'

'You'd be perished!'

'Not really. I'm on leave – from the British Army – home from West Germany on furlough. In fact, I'm on my way to climb the Cairngorm range . . . for a few days.'

'How old are you? the woman asked sharply.

'Twenty-eight, madam. Honestly, I assure you I'm quite used to adverse weather conditions. All part of my training, you know.'

'Are you married?'

'No, madam. I'm a bachelor.' He was slightly surprised by the frank question.

'At your age you ought to be married. I've been married three times. Have you lunched?'

'I had something at the hotel in the village, thank you, madam.'

'Did the hotel people tell you to come here?'

'No, madam. It was entirely my own . . .'

'That's not so bad then. You'd better come inside and have coffee. I notice the Royal Engineers badge on your car.'

'I'm a Sapper sergeant, madam.' And he had an appropriate A.B. 64 in his pocket to prove it if necessary. He produced it for her perusal, but she declined the offer.

'My first husband was a Sapper. Did you know Major Saunders? No, of course you wouldn't, at your age. Do come in and have some coffee.'

'Thank you very much.' MacInnes stood to one side to allow her to precede him into the house. This was going quite well, he thought; perhaps a mite too well. 'This is a very beautiful house,' he said.

'Very expensive to keep going; that's the trouble. I've only one servant, and she's part time. D'you know anything about television sets, Sergeant MacInnes?

'Only to look at, I'm afraid,' he admitted. He followed her into a large lounge where, so evidently, a vast TV set held pride of place. It was the largest set he'd ever seen; and was the single item of modern furniture in the entire room. 'Sorry I can't be of any assistance there.'

'Never mind. D'you smoke?' She offered cigarettes in a silver box, and he accepted one. 'I'm trying to place your accent.'

'I'm a Hebridean, madam.'

'Ah, of course, I ought to have recognized it. D'you speak in Gaelic?'

He nodded, silently. If this majestic female was any kind of criminal, he'd be happy to go out and eat his climbing boots. 'Have you lived here long?'

'Nearly a year. My husband bought the place as an investment. He's off shooting today, actually. I suppose we got a bargain, and with the prices of property rising as they are now, we think it was a very wise move.'

'It most certainly was, madam.'

'Excuse me while I get the coffee. D'you read *The Field*?'

'We get it in the mess from time to time,' he said.

'You'll find copies beside you on the table. For heaven's sake don't disturb their order. My husband's rather touchy about issues being out of sequence.'

He amused himself with the most recent issue of the magazine until the woman returned with the coffee tray. When she appeared, he stood up and returned the magazine to its pile.

'Don't get up, Sergeant. How long d'you want to camp here?'

'Well – for one night . . . if you don't mind.' His last wish was to have to spend a bitterly cold night in a pup tent, but then that was just one other occupational hazard.

'That will be quite all right. My husband will be quite – oh, d'you play bridge?'

'After a fashion, yes, madam.'

'Unless someone turns up, it'll have to be three-handed, of course. D'you mind playing three-handed bridge?

'Not at all, madam.'

MacInnes was suddenly thankful for the small mercy that he could accommodate in this respect. He'd have preferred chess. But he could play bridge with most people, often better than most people. He decided to proceeed delicately.

'When we've had coffee, I'll show you where you can pitch your tent. We have a small meadow on the south side of the house; quite sheltered, too. You ought to be comfortable there. And don't hesitate to come in for anything you need. We put in a water geyser in the summer, so you can have a bath any time you wish.'

'Thank you, madam.' There was nothing else for it now. With a bit of luck there might be a blizzard in the night. That would be perfect, he thought wretchedly. 'Did you know the people who had the Spruces before you came?'

'Not really. It used to belong to one of the Alderton-Fynnes, you know. But they died out and the land agents derived some income by letting it out to holiday people. Some Americans took it – oh, but that's years ago. I haven't an earthly who rented it after them. Yes, I do – sorry about that.'

MacInnes took interest at once. 'Oh, yes?'

'One of the Universities took it for a few months – about two years ago, I think. They ran a sort of educational seminar for visiting students from various countries. I understand that it was quite successful, too. Other than that I haven't a clue, I'm afraid.'

'It must have been a big job to restore,' MacInnes suggested.

'We do it in stages,' the woman explained. 'Still a lot to be done, as you'll understand. The one thing my husband simply will not have is . . . a telephone. I can see his point; after all, he's more or less tied to the phone in the office, and when he comes home it's the last thing he wishes to see. More coffee?'

'Thank you, madam.'

MacInnes felt rather sad. An evening playing bridge with a cranky husband, a night in a cold pup tent, and no means of getting a report back to North Division. And, he suddenly realized, rain was beginning to fall and slash the window glass. W. S. Gilbert had been so right . . . about the Policeman's Lot.

By mid-afternoon Inspector Jumbo Collins had a fairly comprehensive report on Nelson Abney; he also had Abney's form sheet. Thirty-seven years of age, white, five feet seven in height, one hundred and forty pounds, hair brown, eyes brown, spoke in a broad Cockney accent, had a vee-shaped scar on his right buttock, and was known to be left-handed. Collins concentrated on that latter detail.

Watched by Bill Baker, Collins settled himself more firmly in his chair, clenched his left hand into a pistol shooter's grip, swung the hand across his chest, half-turning in the chair, and sighted the invisible pistol to his right, where the equally invisible car window would be. Then he repeated the sighting action with his right hand. It would have been that much easier to fire a pistol with the right hand; but then, he conceded, he was right-handed himself. Collins returned his interest to the Abney form sheet.

Laying that aside he concentrated on the patrol report, as far as it went in the short time allowed for compilation. Abney had arrived in the city three days previously. He had taken up residence at sixty-six Ruby Street, where he occupied a small room on the first floor. His belongings, so far as could be assessed, consisted of one suitcase, a belted tweed overcoat of dark blue material, the clothes he stood up in, and an umbrella. An umbrella . . . Collins rubbed the side of his neck and scowled at the report.

He muttered, half to himself : 'What's a client like Abney wanting with an umbrella, Bill?'

'A brolly can make a very effective weapon, sir; either offensive or defensive. Depends upon how sharp the tip might be,' Baker suggested.

'Ah.' Collins scowled again. 'Organize a warrrant,' he instructed thoughtfully, 'just in case we have to lean on him. Let me have any further information the moment it comes in. We'll go along and discuss the inclement weather with Nelson Abney, I think; you'n me.'

'Right away, sir.' Baker left the office.

The next document had been prepared at great speed, and by a team consisting of detectives, accountants, bank managers, and three eminent stockbrokers. But it gave no information that the Bolesco mob had been indulging themselves in the unpredictable vagaries of the Stock Exchange. A footnote was appended to the effect that the inquiry was continuing as urgently as circumstances permitted.

It was, of course, quite impossible to check thoroughly on the various bookmaking establishments in the city; and it was in those corridors of graft that the real information would almost certainly lie. The Bolesco mob ran no less than three such establishments for a start. The mobs all had similar interests.

Collins placed the Stock Exchange report to one side and took up the next document – a wired copy dealing with the official military career of the recent deceased. Bolesco had been conscripted for army service in 1941. He had received the statutory recruit training and, several months later, had been drafted with his battalion to service in the Far East. Due to an outbreak of dysentry on the troopship, the unit had spent two months in South Africa before proceeding to India. . . . Collins scanned several sentences . . .

In March, 1944, Corporal Bolesco had been parachuted behind the Japanese lines with a special assault force designed to disrupt enemy communications. In the course of an attack on the headquarters of a Japanese brigade, Corporal Bolesco's company had been unexpectedly ambushed by a strong force of the enemy, during which engagement the company commander, two subalterns, and three senior n.c.o.'s had been killed, leaving the remainder of the company in the command of a wounded warrant officer and the corporal concerned. Corporal Bolesco, with notable determination and gallantry, had succeeded in destroying radio communications, killing several of the enemy with grenades, and setting fire to the headquarters hut. By assuming command of the remnants of the small force, and clearing the wounded warrant officer to the rear, he had fought a rearguard action with such ferocity and vigour that the enemy had withdrawn in disorder, allowing the force to dig in and hold their position until reinforced by neighbouring units. For which unremitting gallantry and devotion to duty Corporal Bolesco had been promoted to the rank of sergeant in the field and had later been decorated.

Collins was sufficiently impressed to allow a mild whistle to escape his lips. Automatically, he mentally registered the number of the formation, the date of the action, and the geographical location. Then he placed the report to one side, almost with a sense of reverence.

He was brooding over the fortunes and misfortunes of peace and war when his telephone jerked him back to the present.

'Inspector Collins,' he said sharply into the instrument.

'Sergeant Pearson, sir.'

'Yes, Steve, go ahead.'

'There's some more form come in about Nel Abney. Want me to bring it through?'

'Right away, Steve. Anything interesting?'

'He's supposed to be getting married to some bird on the South Side, sir. Day after tomorrow, according to the tip-off.'

'Bring it through, anyway. Check back on it when you can.'

Pearson entered the office and gave Collins the hastily scribbled notes, mentioning the name of his informant.

'Could be it's real, Steve.' The informant mentioned had always been very reliable. 'Keep him working on it; and see he gets paid.'

'Aye, sure thing, Jumbo.'

'Did you read Tony's war record?'

'Aye, I did that.'

'You know more about it than I can ever know.' Collins' eyes were on the red, white and blue ribbon of the M.M. that headed the sergeant's decorations. 'It must have been bloody terrible, that.'

'Better him than me,' Pearson admitted. 'You can keep the jungle, and the Japs, too, s'far's I'm concerned.'

'The poor bastard,' Collins muttered; 'the poor, stupid big bastard . . .'

10

Rimmer and Pixie Greer heard the engines of the motor-cycles several seconds before the machines were sweeping into the entry of the Braid Street lock-up yard. There were four machines, aboard two of which rode pillion passengers. The riders were all male, young, long-haired, leather jacketed, but to the two hidden observers behind the rickety double doors, unfamiliar. The youths dismounted and propped their bikes on stands. A few minutes were spent in discussing their proposed activities for the coming weekend. Then the riders produced cloths and cans of metal cleaner and got down to the essential task of polishing.

One of the pillion passengers went across the yard to where a water tap had been mounted against a concrete post, soaked the cloth he was carrying, wrung it out, and returned to work on the muddy under-frame of his host machine.

Greer whispered: 'Don't know how you feel about it, Dick, but I get the signal that these kids are square enough.'

'Maybe; maybe it's a front. Seen any of them before?'

'No. Probably in from the country. There's a football match on tonight at Caledon Park.'

'I see how you figure it,' Rimmer said, nodding. One of the enthusiasts was wearing a pair of nearly new soccer boots. 'You could have it there. I'll take the numbers, to be on the safe side later on.' Rimmer noted the registrations and the model brand names.

The youths, except for the occasional remark about the work in hand, indulged in their tasks with notable diligence. The moment a particular part of the machine was cleaned, it was scrupulously examined and, where it was felt necessary, was treated to a fine spray of protecting fluid from an aerosol container. Greer noted this with approval. The kids obviously had a great pride in their bikes. That, to his way of reasoning, tended to put them on creditable side of his personal column of estimation. And despite the flowing locks, they were all clean, their footwear polished, their faces shaved. Greer didn't anticipate any trouble from this small gang of lads. Through the vertical aperture between the doors, he could see Dusty Miller in the Wolseley, smoking a cigarette and reading a newspaper.

'About time we checked transmission, Dickie boy,' he whispered.

'Just going to do that very thing.' Rimmer held the mini-ature walkie-talkie close to his mouth and said softly : 'Dee to Dee, over.'

'I get you okay, Dick, over.'

'Checking as arranged, over.'

'Who are the yobbos with the road-burners?' Miller asked.

'You tell me, mate,' Rimmer said. 'Recognize any of them?'

'Not really. Got their numbers?'

'What d'*you* think, Sherlock?'

'Might be an opening gambit.'

'As if you would know about opening gambits,' Rimmer said sourly, recalling the thrashing meted out by MacInnes earlier that morning.

'Might be, though,' Miller persisted. 'I'm ringing in to Divi-sion . . .'

'Hold it for a few minutes. We don't want a bunch of uni-formed zombies switching on yet.'

'Holding, over.'

'What's the street like out there?'

'Two wifies with prams, a nifty looker at the door of fifty-four, and Robbie massaging the window glass directly above her.'

'She looking up his trouser leg, by any chance?' Rimmer asked.

'Could be. She's chatting him up, anyway.'

'It's what comes of being young, handsome and well blessed. What's the odds that Robbie gets . . .'

'Hello, Dee to Dee,' Miller said urgently. 'What's up? Over.'

Rimmer and Greer watched one of the youths moving in the direction of their lock-up. Rimmer said swiftly: 'This just might be it. Stay with me. Over.'

The youth approached leisurely, his eyes sweeping the line of lock-ups in front of him. He was one of the two pillion passengers. They heard the doors of the next lock-up rattle as the youth tried the lock. Greer held the large cabinet screwdriver ready to rip away the slackened screws in the upper hinge. Rimmer glanced through the aperture in the direction of the Wolseley. Dusty continued to hold the newspaper across the steering wheel, but his head had moved slightly to the right.

Several moments later the double doors of the lock-up shook noisily. Greer kept the screwdriver poised beside the upper hinge. The other members of the gang were still busily engaged in the bull session on the bikes in the centre of the yard. 'Hey, lads,' the youth called to them, 'see this door here; they're hanging off the hinges.' He shook the doors again. 'What about a look inside, eh?'

'Come on out of there,' one of the others replied. 'That's the road you get into a lot of bad trouble, Happy. Come on, and don't be so bloomin' daft.'

Greer was furiously tightening the hinge screws, as the doors shook again. One of the screws in the lower hinge had jumped free of its socket and had rolled out of sight. Greer was on his knees working on the other two.

'No harm in having a wee look inside,' the youth called over his shoulder. 'The doors are hanging off – like as not there's nothing in the shed.'

'If there's nothing in the shed, there's no sense in looking inside it then.'

Another suggested: 'No sense in not looking for nothing.'

'No harm in having . . .' the youth shook the doors again more strenuously this time '. . . that's funny.'

'What's funny, Happy? Tell me and I'll laugh my head off. But tell me.' A tall blond boy threw back his head and said: 'Ha, ha,' very solemnly.

'Must've got jammed on something,' the inquisitive member muttered, again shaking the doors. 'I couldn've swore they was loose when I tried them first.'

'Well then, knock it off, Happy.'

'Och, I wasn't meaning to . . .'

'Come on, it's getting on for half three. Let's get moving down the road.' The speaker kicked his bike into life, revving the engine gently.

The others were stowing their cleaning materials into side pannier bags strapped to the rear frames. 'Come on, lads. This is us for the match.'

'We've plenty of time for the match,' Happy said truculently. 'I wasn't meaning any harm at all. It was just that them doors was . . .'

'Ach, put your tongue in your pocket and get up here on my pillion. Come on, you big stumer, or else you walk.'

Happy decided that riding pillion was better than walking.

Less than a minute later the yard was empty of life, the smooth rumble of big twin engines gradually fading with the distance.

Rimmer said: 'I could do with a pint.'

Greer nodded and pulled the package of rations between them. 'Maybe they packed a few cans of beer for us.'

But, of course, they hadn't. There was no beer, only a thermos of coffee. But there was no beer.

So they waited inside the lock-up for the next thing to happen.

In the Wolseley, Dusty Miller yawned and thought about Slim Summerville. The window cleaner was back on the ground, his right elbow jammed into a space in his ladder. He was chatting up the nifty looker on the doorstep of fifty-four.

Sometimes, for some, Miller reflected, the job had its moments.

Bill Baker was on his way from the canteen to his office, a mug of tea in one hand and a hot sausage roll wrapped in a serviette in the other, when he was intercepted by Steve Pearson carrying a scribbled report from Hamish MacInnes.

'Jumbo about, Bill?' Pearson asked him.

'He went out to congratulate Nel Abney on his nuptials.' Baker took on a section of hot sausage roll and chewed on it delicately.

'I can imagine,' the sergeant said, opening the office door for Baker. 'Anybody go with him?'

'One of the crews; don't know which. Jumbo's got a warrant with him. Wants to inspect the plumbing, or something.' Baker put the tea mug on his desk and held his hand out for the report. 'What's this then, Steve?'

'MacInnes rang in from Strath Garry. Looks like he's stuck up there for the night. Spending the evening playing bridge with the local laird and his lady.'

'At a time like this – playing bridge. I don't know . . .' he scanned the notes slowly. 'What's this mean . . . either Mrs. or Miss?'

'The Sinclair piece. He managed to get some griff from the local chemist. Seems Joy Sinclair bought some dope for bronchitis at the chemist's shop and was asked to sign the poison register.'

'I see that. But it's doubtful if she was a married lady or an allegedly chaste virgin . . . is that it?'

'She's a bad writer,' Pearson said. 'Hamish had a hell of a job to read what she had signed; that's what it was. But she was the Sinclair piece all right. The chemist recognized her right away.'

Baker glanced at the report again. 'So she signed herself in the poison register as either Miss or Mrs. Ross.'

'That's what our highland laddie reported, Bill. He had to make an excuse to go into the village for fags or something, because the laird is a crank who can't bear to have the phone in his house. This would have been here hours ago otherwise.'

'Miss or Mrs. Ross,' Baker muttered. 'See what you can find on her.'

'I did. Joy Sinclair was married at seventeen, to some Eyetie client who decided to forget about her for the sunny slopes of Vesuvius. But she was born and baptized as Sinclair, back in 'forty-three. I got on to the Central Registry about it.'

'Any griff on her using an alias of Ross in the past, besides this?'

'Nothing at all. No report of her using an alias any time, Bill.'

'Interesting,' Baker observed, 'but I can't see it slotting in anywhere. Any suggestions?'

'Nothing coming through at all, Bill.'

'What've we got on her so far?'

'First a charge of soliciting, September 'sixty-four: driving without licence or insurance, May 'sixty-six: shoplifting, August 'sixty-nine. Fined on each conviction.' Pearson rattled off the information without hesitation. He had, in fact, handled the shoplifting case himself.

'All minor stuff,' Baker mused. 'What was the date on that poison register again?' He consulted the report and said: 'December eighteenth, nineteen seventy. Umhum. So she was involved in some deal in Strath Garry around Christmas of 'seventy. Get on to County and see if they can dig up anything that might tie in, Steve.' He paused and counted back in time. 'Tony Bolesco would have been into what – about the second year of his sentence around that time? Right?'

'Near enough.' The sergeant made a note on a pad, and said: 'Shouldn't take us very long. I'll get on to County now.'

Baker nodded absently, and the sergeant left the office.

Baker remembered the remains of the hot sausage roll and, chewing reflectively, stared unseeingly down on the street outside.

The world was full of trouble.

Collins watched the last of the afternoon visitors leaving the hospital, the rain gusting in flurries against the windows of his car as the daylight began to yield to the gathering dusk. He hadn't gone anywhere near Nel Abney that day. Better that he left the gunman's surveillance to the circumspect attentions of his informant and to a brace of female specialists in that field. He was going to play this show in one of his occasionally unorthodox ways. There would be no information forthcoming from any member of the Bolesco mob, or from any member of the other mobs. So he was going to try his luck in another direction.

When he felt convinced that the visitors had been cleared of the wards, he locked the car and made his way up the broad flight of stone steps and introduced himself to the receptionist.

The girl consulted her register and said: 'Ward Eight, Inspector; second floor. Father Cabrelli's waiting for you in the Sister's office.'

Collins nodded thanks and climbed the stairs, hopefully, yet somewhat doubtfully. When he had asked the priest's indulgence in the matter he had wondered whether it would have been prudent. But the priest had proved to be more amenable. Collins found the cleric to be quite a young man, with an odd intense personality, whether severe or approving he could not tell.

'I'm very grateful . . .' he began to say as they shook hands.

'You mustn't stay very long, Inspector,' the priest murmured.

'No, of course not. I understand he's very low.'

'One can never tell. If you wish I shall talk to him . . .'

'I'll be guided by you in every respect, Father.' Collins then asked: 'Does he know – about . . . how his son died?'

'I decided to tell him. Better that it came from me than from others. At this stage it can make little difference, Inspector.'

Collins nodded, approving the priest's practical attitude. He waited outside the ward door for several minutes until Father Cabrelli came to signal him to follow.

Guido Bolesco had been propped up in bed. Collins had the almost shattering impression that he was able to see right through the old man, there was so little left on his frame. But the large black eyes were full of light, unwinking, holding, firing out some sort of invisible challenge like shells from twin cannon.

Collins sat on the chair where the priest indicated, close to the dying patient. In a humble voice he said: 'I'm Inspector Collins, Mr. Bolesco. I've come to ask you to help me to find the people who – to find out why your son . . .'

'*Mio figlio era molto gentile. Tutti che conoscervano lui volesterono bene.*' Guido Bolesco's voice was faint, but sufficiently articulate to follow.

Collins glanced at the priest in confusion. The priest said: 'My son was a very kind boy. Everybody he knew was happy with him, and very fond of him.' To the patient he said: 'The inspector would be happy if you speak in English, Guido.'

'I am sorry,' the patient said softly. 'Tony was a good boy to us, he gave us many nice things.'

'Yes, Mr. Bolesco,' Collins said, 'I knew about that.' Glancing across at he priest he said: 'If you could tell me about anybody who did not like him, I might be able to . . .'

'Everybody like my Tony,' Guido Bolesco said weakly. 'Inna war he get a great medal. He come home and give me his medal. The soldiers also like . . .' the voice stopped suddenly.

'Wait, Inspector,' Father Cabrelli said gently.

Collins nodded silently and waited.

Presently the patient lay back and closed his great dark eyes. Then he said: *'Io mi ricordo, uno volta quando veni questo uomo, a vedere mio figlio. Mi ricordo di lui, perché aveva una mano ferita.'*

'Guido,' the priest said, 'the inspector does not . . .'

'It's perfectly all right, Father,' Collins interrupted gently. 'If you'll translate for me, please.'

'I remember there was one time when this man came to see my son.' The priest translated slowly and very clearly. 'I remember him because of the sore hand.'

'The . . . sore hand, Father?'

'Sì,' the patient interposed weakly. 'That is right. The sorr 'and. Ver' sorr 'and.'

Collins thought about it and dared to inquire. 'This man had a sore hand . . . because of fighting — because he and your son had a fight?'

'Una mano ferita, sì. Una mano ferita dalla guerra.'

'A sore hand,' the priest repeated. 'From the war.'

'Quando si vení qui molto tempo fa. Io lo sapeste che si sarebbe stato molto felici qua, perché mio figlio faceva tutto per noi, era un ragazzo molto intelligente. Luih imparo la lingua inglese in poco tempo per ché lui era così giovane . . .'

Collins shook his head at the priest. 'I managed to catch some of that. Tony speak English very quickly . . . yes?'

'Yes. You are very quick, Inspector.'

'About this man with the sore hand, Father.'

'Nothing.'

Collins allowed his tongue to explore the cavity between his teeth. A sore hand . . . from the war. A war wound. Tony had been in the war. Both men had been in the war. Who

144

had done the wounding? The enemy? Self-inflicted? He gave it another minute before continuing.

'Mr. Bolesco, this man with the sore hand, and your son Tony; did they like each other? Were they friends?'

'No, not friends. They not friends. All other soldiers Tony's friends. They come to see us at my house. All friends to Tony. This one not friend anyhow.' Then the patient began to speak very quickly in Italian, so softly that Collins failed to hear it properly. But the priest had quickly leaned close and was nodding encouragingly as he listened.

'I think the ward sister's coming this way, Father,' Collins said.

'I can see her in the mirror there. We have . . .' Father Cabrelli stood up and smiled at the smartly uniformed girl. 'We are just going, Sister.'

'Two minutes, gentlemen,' she said, and moved smartly down the line of beds.

'What was all that, Father?' Collins asked.

'This man came to their house. He had some sort of legal order – I think that's what Guido meant. He was going to take action against Tony for the damage to his hand. That's the best I can do, I'm afraid.'

'You've done very well, indeed,' Collins lied evenly. 'Ask him if this client – if this man and Tony were in the war together – in the same formation, or unit. Can you do that?'

But the patient forestalled them '*Io penso che lui conosceva mio figlio in tempo di guerra, si. Io penso che fossero in combattimento tutti due insieme.*'

'That could mean yes to my question,' Collins tried.

'He thinks so, yes. He thinks that this man and Tony were fighting together during the war.'

'Where, Father?' Collins asked. 'In which theatre of war?'

The priest inquired, but the patient didn't know.

The ward sister sister was back with them. They bade the

patient farewell, Collins shook the old withered hand and promised to do all he could to find a satisfactory answer to the matter, telling the patient that he had been very helpful in the inquiry. But Collins couldn't find himself meaning all of that. Men with sore hands were to be met at every other street corner. And over twenty-five years had elapsed since, apparently, that sore hand had – or may have been – the sole clue to the investigation.

Going down the stairs, Collins asked the priest: 'Can I drive you home – anywhere – Father?'

'I have another patient to visit before I can leave, Inspector.'

'I can wait if you wish. What else can I do to repay you for all you have done for me? Without your assistance . . .'

'Why else would I live my life?' the priest asked evenly.

'Yes, indeed. Why else, Father?'

'May I ask if you feel hopeful with what he have . . .'

'Not very hopeful, Father. I wouldn't try and lie to you at a time like this. But then, I'm only one member of the organization. By the time I get back to my office, one of my colleagues may have unearthed another item – we might knit both items together – the man with the sore hand and this second item . . . who knows, Father?'

'You may call on me at any time, Inspector,' the priest said, holding out his right hand.

Shaking it firmly, Collins said: 'I may have to, Father. If I ring you in the morning, could you find the time to come back here with me? Should there be something I have foolishly forgotten?'

'You are not a foolish man, Inspector. Ring me at any time.'

'Thank you. Perhaps in the morning, then.'

The priest watched Collins putting on his hat and turning up the collar of his overcoat and, thinking about the patient in the second floor ward, he said quietly: '*Deo volente*, Inspector.'

Collins got the point. He nodded: *'Deo volente*, Father.'

Then he went downstairs and drove back to North Division.

Unknown to Collins, a colleague *had* unearthed another item back at North Division.

I I

Collins parked his car in the yard behind North Division H.Q. and passed a few moments in the interested study of two uniformed men who were then engaged in carrying cardboard cubes from a closed van, one of three, into the rear entrance of the grey building on the upper floor of which was his personal office. The cardboard cubes were, in the rapidly fading light of the late afternoon, obviously packed cases of, at a guess, booze of some description. The uniformed men were capless, tunicless, and sweating slightly. Collins got out of his car and intercepted the taller of the two.

With his hands deep in the pockets of his overcoat, and the brim of his hat forward over his brow, he asked: 'What's this, then?'

The uniformed man, less than a month out of initial training and still of a mind that the local operative D.I. was God's immediate hatchetman – and *not* just another old hairy-arsed, disgruntled, embittered, thoroughly scunnered beetle-crushing bastard – stood stiffly to attention under his load of confiscated whisky, and answered: 'It's . . . whisky, sir.'

'Am I invited, Constable?'

'Invited, sir?'

'You're having a party, I presume . . . in there.' Collins jerked his head in the direction of the rear entrance to North Division.

'Well, sir . . . that is – no, sir. We're moving this evidence . . .'

'Evidence? Case of whisky? Bless my soul,' Collins said.

'From Braid Street, sir.'

'Ah. Braid Street. How'd it happen?'

'D.C. Rimmer, sir. He – that is, we – when D.C. Rimmer . . .'

'Went out to recover cases of whisky. I see, Constable. Well, fair enough then. Carry on.'

'Er . . . yes, sir.' The young constable tottered off with his burden of the joys of life. His immediate thoughts were quite unprintable. The young constable was learning his trade quickly.

Collins stood beside the closed vans, noting that but one had been unlocked. Dick Rimmer had done a good job. Might be worth while having a look at the other exhibits. Collins moved through the rear entrance and eventually into the charge room.

Steve Pearson, his facial expression as bored as usual, was writing details in a ledger. Four males, all white, all comparatively young, were lined up on one side of the counter, handcuffed one to the other. Collins mentally remarked on the slightly disfigured countenance of one, the smear of dried blood that filigreed from the left corner of the mouth of another, and the gradually swelling eyes of a third. Dick Rimmer, he also noted, had had his collar disarranged, and the knuckles of his right hand had been temporarily bandaged with a handkerchief. Collins examined the faces of the captives, but failed to recognize any one of them. New clients – new clients making a big début into the trade.

Pixie Greer was sitting on a stool, smoking a somewhat filthy dog-end, and observing the official procedure from a safe distance.

Collins asked the little man: 'Have a nice time?'

'Not bad, sir.' Greer stood up as he was spoken to. 'Braid Street lock-ups job. Went down a treat.'

'What happened to laughing boy there?' Collins indicated the youth with the gradually swelling orbs.

'Walked into the edge of a lock-up, sir.'

'Really? Walked into a door? Well, well, well.'

'Getting dark at the time, sir,' Greer explained.

'Of course. I should have known. Bill Baker about?'

'I think you'll find him in your own office, sir,' Greer said.

'Ah.' Collins walked out of the charge room thoughtfully. A short visit to Frank Wishart in the morning. A personal recommendation – with the *very* utmost respect – in so many words . . . Dick Rimmer was so long overdue for promotion, if the self-centred, soured idiot would accept it . . . and then back to the job of trying to solve the Bolesco assassination.

Bill Baker was scrutinizing the daily copy of the official police publication when Collins entered the office. The D.C. put it to one side and stood up at his desk.

'What's it look like today, Bill?' Collins referred to the daily publication.

'Mostly on the London bombers, sir. Couple of travellers on the move from Birmingham on the way north. And the Viscount's been liberated from Durham.'

'How nice for the Viscount. I'll give him a month before he's right back in there.' Collins made the prediction with conviction.

The Viscount, a sophisticated – or contra-sophisticated – conman, seldom went for more than a couple of weeks before someone caught up with him. One of Nature's most determined idiots. Collins asked Baker for the name of the travellers, and thought about them. Both were Scots by birth, both white; one dangerous, the other a poof and a fairly experienced burglar. Collins nodded and glanced at his in tray, removed his overcoat, hung it on a peg, and went to stare down at the wet street outside from the window. He remained in that posture for more than a minute, while Baker stood waiting.

'Bill,' Collins said eventually, 'I went to see Tony Bolesco's old dad this afternoon. He told me about a client with a sore hand. *Una mano ferita*. Somewhere, some time, between yesterday and . . . God knows when. Twenty goodness knows how many years ago. Everybody liked Tony . . .

and I think I can understand that. Oddly enough, I sort of liked the big stupid bastard myself. That war record. Bags of sheer guts and determination. You can't help liking a client like that – when he's got his own share of courage and your own as well . . . am I making any sense to you, Bill?' Collins continued to stare down at the wet street outside.

'I think so, sir. I read the Defence Ministry report, too.'

'This client with the sore hand *didn't* like Tony,' Collins said. 'Who're we looking for, Bill?'

'I don't have a single idea, sir,' Baker admitted helplessly.

'Nor I,' Collins muttered, half to himself.

'Hamish MacInnes rang in a report from Strath Garry. Looks as if Joy Sinclair was living up there in nineteen-seventy, Christmas time, posing as a Miss or Mrs. Ross. We checked with County on anything significant in that area, but County couldn't produce as much as a single word. No trouble in Strath Garry during Christmas of 'seventy. Nothing at all.'

'*Una mano ferita,*' Collins repeated thoughtfully.

'And there's a flimsy from Doc Cameron, sir.'

'About what; about whom, rather?'

'You asked for a medical report on one of the regulars who nipped in to confess to the Bolesco shooting.'

Collins half-turned from the window, paused, let his face go lop-sided, and nodded. 'So I did, Bill. So I did.'

'It's right here, sir.' Baker offered the enveloped flimsy.

Collins was smiling thinly as he accepted it.

The voice that answered the telephone call said: 'Sergeant Main, Forensic Department.'

'Inspector Collins, George.'

'Oh, yes, sir. I was just about to knock off.'

'Before you do, George, I'd be grateful if you'd confirm one item. About that Jap automatic pistol. That seven milli-metre Nambu.'

'Yes, sir. No bother at all. What did you want to know?'

'Would that model of Nambu automatic have been in general circulation at or before the spring of nineteen forty-four?'

'Hang on, I'll have a look in the big book.'

Collins hung on. He hung on for at least four minutes.

Then the voice of the forensic sergeant said: 'I can't answer the specific question with any accuracy. The Nambu was developed – and I quote – before the outbreak of the Second World War. That statement refers, as I read it, to the *eight* millimetre model. At the same time, the way the literature goes, it could also refer to the seven millimetre job. At a guess I'd say the seven mil job was in circulation in nineteen forty-four, sir.'

'It seems reasonable, then, George?' Collins asked.

'To me, yes. Incidentally, I can arrange for a specimen to be sent up from Metropolitan. They hold one on reference.'

'Well done,' Collins said approvingly. 'Leave it for the moment. I'll be in touch with you if I need that model.'

'Righto, sir. Having luck, are we?'

'Maybe, George. Maybe.' Collins hung up his telephone and smiled benignly at Bill Baker.

Baker expressed open concern: it was a part of his professional training, but it didn't fool Collins. 'Sir?'

'Come off it, Bill. I learned to do that before you came up.'

'Do what, sir?'

'Don't give me that,' Collins said sharply.

'No, sir. I apologize. Anything I ought to know?'

'I think,' Collins intimated softly: 'I think we've got him.'

But they hadn't; not really.

They took their time about approaching number eighteen King Harald Street. They had prepared no plan of operation. It was simply to be another inquiry. Collins carried an official search warrant on his person. Neither he nor Baker carried arms. They did not anticipate any violence. Behind them, a uniformed patrol car driver edged the blue car against the kerb, between a Bentley Continental and a vintage Lea Francis. The driver switched off the ignition, watched Collins and Baker eventually mount the flight of steps leading up to the large apartmented house, and then surreptitiously lit a cigarette, watching his rear in the driving mirror as he did so. Across the street a party of young people were getting into a minibus on their way to some function or other. The driver settled back in his seat and inhaled deeply from the cigarette in his cupped hand. Collins and Baker had disappeared into the house.

The apartment occupied by James Craig Rose was on the second floor. Collins studied the heavy panelled puce-coloured door for a few seconds before thumbing the bell push. A two-toned gong-like sound filtered back to them as they waited.

When Rose answered the summons, Collins said: 'Good evening, Mr. Rose. This is Detective Constable Baker and we . . .'

'And who are you?' Rose asked blankly.

'I am . . . Inspector Collins, sir,' Collins said patiently.

'Indeed? Have you some form of identification?'

Collins produced his warrant card silently and waited until Rose had satisfied himself that the caller was genuine. 'We hoped you . . .'

'And yours, my good man?' Rose demanded of Baker.

The charade was repeated silently.

'Mr. Rose,' Collins informed him, 'we have come to ask if you will cooperate in our inquiries regarding the death of Anthony Bolesco. May we come in?'

'No reason why not.' Rose stood to one side and let them pass into the apartment, closing the puce-coloured door after them. 'Will the lounge suit you?'

'I'm sure the lounge will be adequate, sir,' Collins said.

The lounge was a large, high ceilinged room, expensively decorated and furnished with carefully chosen antique pieces to such a degree that Bill Baker was at a loss to decide whether this was a room to be lived in or to be lived with. Rose neglected to invite them to be seated, so all three stood while Collins opened the interview.

Before the inspector got under way, Rose asked: 'Doesn't one get cautioned first of all?'

'Not necessarily, sir,' Collins said. There were two sides to the matter of a caution: the moment a suspect was cautioned, no further questions were permitted; and a statement without intimation of a preliminary caution would be thrown out of court. Collins wondered just how much Rose might know about these points. 'We would be grateful if you'd answer a few questions, that's all.'

'Do please proceed, Inspector,' Rose said, simpering.

'You will remember being in my office yesterday, sir?'

'Will I? Perhaps I was. Why?'

'You may recall telling me that you had shot Anthony Bolesco yesterday at ten-forty-five in the morning.'

'Perhaps I did,' Rose half admitted. 'I'm a very good shot.'

'You told me that as well,' Collins said, making a note.

'Don't you have your assistant do the donkey work?'

'Donkey work, Mr. Rose?' Collins expressed surprise.

'Making the notes and so on.'

'Mr. Baker did the notes yesterday. It's my turn today.'

Rose beamed momentarily. 'How very democratic!'

'Yes, sir. As you say.' Collins struggled to remain calm. 'You said you fired two or three shots, I think.'

'You have a good memory,' Rose complimented him. 'D'you remember what I did with the gun?'

'You dropped it in the river at North Bridge, sir, according to . . .'

'How right you are.' Rose permitted a small chuckle to escape.

'Can you describe the gun, sir?'

'Service revolver. One of the early ones.'

'One of . . . the early ones? How early, sir?'

'Oh, how do I know? Aren't your frogmen going to dive in and fetch it up?' Rose's voice held a haughty note.

'D'you know what make it was?' Collins persisted evenly.

'Haven't a clue, dear man. Six shooter type of revolver. It holds six cartridges. I had it in the war, you know. I was an officer. Did you know that, Inspector? I was a lieutenant; first lieutenant.'

'I know that, Mr. Rose.'

'Really? My goodness, you *have* been a busy man.'

From his position slightly behind Rose, Bill Baker watched the man's confident poise. There was no evidence of strain about him. Rose was, so far as Baker could judge, thoroughly composed . . . and shifty.

'I also know that you were dropped behind the Japanese lines by parachute in the month of March, 1944, and that you were severely wounded in the ensuing action during which . . .'

'I was left for dead, Inspector,' Rose told him. 'But I didn't die. Instead I was taken as a prisoner of war by the Japanese.'

'Who subjected you to torture during interrogation.'

Rose clenched his fists. 'They scorched my hands with a red hot bayonet . . . as perhaps you can see.' He held both his hands out for their inspection. 'Hardly a pleasant experience.'

Collins made more notes. 'But you managed to keep your service revolver . . .'

'I didn't say that, Inspector,' Rose protested.

Collins read the shorthand symbols he had made. 'Quote – It holds six cartridges. I had it in the war, you know . . .'

'What I meant to say was that I had one like it. After I was liberated I volunteered to serve in an administrative capacity. Consequently I was reissued with a similar revolver.'

'I see, sir.'

'You must be careful about details, you know,' Rose said primly, and simpered again. 'Easy to make mistakes.'

'The reissued revolver was a – of British make?'

'Naturally! What else would it be? I was a British officer.'

'Did you ever take possession of a Japanese pistol . . . from an enemy prisoner, for example?'

'Good heavens, what would one do with such a thing?' Rose chuckled again. 'Aren't you being rather facetious?'

Collins tried another tack. 'In the same formation there was an n.c.o., Corporal Anthony Bolesco, I think.'

'My dear man, the formation comprised over five hundred troops. How would I know who the junior n.c.o.'s were?'

Still no sign of strain, Baker noted.

Collins tried a third tack. 'Can you remember where you were during the Christmas period of nineteen seventy, sir?'

'Very clearly. I rented a house in Strath Garry. The Spruces. This flat was being redecorated and I decided to rent the place for a few weeks while the work was being carried out. Very restful; delightful district.'

'Did you live at the Spruces alone, sir?'

'I had my man with me, of course. Rodney's out today.'

'Just the two of you, living at the Spruces?'

'Not always, Inspector. I threw a few parties . . . for business associates and friends, you know. We had some very jolly parties at the Spruces. I like to have lots and lots of people at Christmas.'

Collins nodded agreeably. It could be checked, but it would take time. 'Yes, sir, naturally. D'you remember a lady by the name of Joy Sinclair being at the Spruces about that time?'

'Can't say I do, really. The house was packed with people. I mean to say, you know, these were *real* parties. Dozens and dozens of people and friends. Not everyone has the wherewithal to . . .'

'Have you ever frequented the Crystal Club in town, sir?'

'May have done. Couldn't really say. I suppose one gets round most of the night spots in town over the years. One's so much like another. In fact, I was invited to some club only last month, but for the life of me I couldn't tell you which one, or even where it might be.'

'Quite, sir. Night clubs do occasionally tend to fade from the memory after a gay evening.'

Rose simpered and nodded. 'I'm rather susceptible to a couple of drinks too many, Inspector.'

'Aren't we all,' Collins conceded, making another note. 'You cannot recall Corporal Bolesco being in your formation in . . .'

'Would he have been some relation to the fellow who smashed into the omnibus yesterday?'

'The same man.'

'Good heavens, how very extraordinary.'

'Extraordinary?' Collins waited patiently.

'Don't *you* think so?'

'During the action behind the enemy lines, sir . . .'

'I'd rather forget all that, dear man. It wasn't funny.' Rose's voice rose sharply. 'You wouldn't understand, not having been engaged in warfare. You're too young; too callow, Inspector. We – who have – never forget it; but we spend the remainder of our lives trying to forget it.'

Collins decided to put the boot in, gently. He kept his eyes on Bill Baker, who winked in reply for his position behind Rose. 'According to the information I have, Mr. Rose, you spent a number of weeks undergoing psychiatric treatment in . . .'

'What business is that of yours?' Rose retorted hotly.

'It is, nevertheless, true, sir?'

'Of course it's true. So, too, did hundreds of servicemen who suffered – suffered for people like you, I might add. Have you ever suffered like we did? Of course you didn't. Neither one of you.' Rose clenched his fists again, looked down at his mutilated hands, and held them out at arm's length. 'Do you have scars like these? Well, do you?'

'How did you get wounded, sir?' Baker asked quietly from behind him. The signal that had passed from Collins indicated to Baker to continue until Collins had time to consider the situation.

'By a Japanese mortar shell fragment.' He bowed his head and parted the carefully arranged hair, so that they could see the indentation on the top of his skull. 'I must have been one of the first to fall. But I didn't die. I was alive – unconscious, but alive!' Rose said expansively. 'Oh yes, they couldn't break me!'

Collins tried to recall the nature of Bolesco's military report. The force had been attacked . . . but Bolesco's fierce counter measures had held the position until reinforcements had come up . . . if Rose had been left for dead, and the position had been held by the remnants of the force, how had it come about that Rose had been taken by the Japs? Something didn't quite click there. Nevertheless, Rose had been taken prisoner. That was official enough, anyway.

Baker was asking him: 'Were you unconscious for a long time?'

'How the devil would I know that? We didn't have the benefit of calendars, young man. We didn't have the benefit of hospital theatres either, unless you . . .'

'What colour is your car, Mr. Rose?' Baker inquired.

'My car? Colour? What bearing has the colour of my . . .'

'It might help us in our inquiries,' Baker explained quietly.

'The colour is known as almond green, I believe.'

'Thank you.' Baker caught Collins' eye and desisted.

Collins had to proceed with caution. Doctor Cameron's flimsy had given only basic details. Medical histories were treated with essential confidence in the profession; unless, of course, a suspect had been cautioned, charged and held in custody for further examination. All the flimsy had indicated was that Rose had been taken as a prisoner of war by the Japanese, had been interrogated under torture, as a result of which he had undergone psychiatric treatment afterwards. From those few details, Collins had endeavoured to form a fuller picture, accurate or otherwise.

He had already noted the haughty, expansive character of the suspect; and wondered how much of it might have been genuine and how much might have been bluff. If it was bluff, Rose was carrying it off very convincingly.

'Mr. Rose, you needn't answer my next question if you . . .'

'I shall do my best to answer any question you present,' Rose said sharply. 'I'm a decent citizen. Why shouldn't I . . .'

'Did you receive a disability pension after . . .'

'A pittance, Inspector. I never complained about it. But I deserved much more than I got. We all did. Look what I missed by being in captivity. I might have – I *would* have reached field rank at least. I'm not altogether an idiot, you know. Look what I have achieved since then. I could buy and sell both of you. A dozen times over.'

'What is the make of your car, sir?' Collins asked evenly.

'I run a small town car, an Audi.'

'Almond green in colour?'

'I can't see why you continue to dwell on . . .'

'Perhaps not, sir. Almond green in colour?'

'Yes. I also have a limousine for touring – a Bentley.'

'The Continental model outside?'

'D'you honestly believe that I'd leave a Bentley in the street, Inspector? With all the vandalism we have to bear to-day? D'you really believe I'm completely stupid?'

Collins went through the motions of making a note. When Rose had left North Division headquarters, he had taken a taxi home. But he ran an expensive Audi for jazzing round the town, and had a Bentley tucked away to keep the town car company in some garage in the vicinity. He made a genuine note then – to check whether this client had had his licence suspended under Section Six. Perhaps this Rodney client did the driving for him . . . Rodney could be dealt with at a later date.

'Mr. Rose,' he said eventually, 'would you recognize a

photograph of Bolesco?'

'How on earth would I know, Inspector?'

Behind the suspect, Baker pulled a rueful expression. But Collins was more optimistic. He stated: 'You must have recognized him in the car when you shot him, sir; yesterday morning.'

'People are very difficult to recognize in cars,' Rose said. 'I mean to say – haven't you noticed that, Inspector?'

Containing his patience, Collins produced the clinical prints of the cadaver with the shot marks in its neck and offered them.

Rose examined the close-ups. 'Yes, that's the man, I think.' He looked closer, and smiled. 'I did very well, indeed, didn't I? Very accurate shooting. I told you I was an expert shot. Of course, I was out of practice, after all the years. But I certainly can shoot extremely well. I'm a natural, you know.'

'You did tell me that, sir.' Collins retrieved the photographs and returned them to his pocket.

'Of course, he smashed into the omnibus,' Rose said suddenly.

'The omnibus, sir?'

'That's what really killed him.'

'How d'you make that out?'

'Bound to have done!' Rose's voice rose half an octave. 'A smash like that – broken glass, smashed body work. Have you ever seen a smash like that? I've seen one: I've seen hundreds! I've seen the angels of death in the jungle, Inspector. Black angels, with palm fronds in their hands . . . waving palm fronds, slowly, overhead in the sky. The symbols of retribution.' Rose began to pace up and down the room; six steps in one direction, six in the other. As he walked, he held his hands out in front, palms outermost, about a foot apart. 'Retribution. Nobody can escape in the end. One lives and one dies. But never without retribution for . . .'

'Mr. Rose!' Collins said sharply.

'Don't you dare shout at me . . . in my own house. I own this house, remember. *I* am the owner. I don't – I'm not like you. I paid for this house, with honestly earned money. I don't have a rent book. I don't have to live in a police cottage, Inspector. I could buy a dozen houses like this.'

'We're getting away from the point,' Collins told him, nearing the end of his patience.

'I said I would answer any question you chose to present, didn't I? I told you that less than a minute ago. Didn't you hear?'

'Why did you shoot Bolesco, sir?' Collins tried, prepared for anything now.

'Because he left me for dead in the jungle. Because he was responsible for – these!' Rose held out his mutilated hands. 'I had to suffer. I bore the red hot bayonets. I had to suffer, but I continued to live. I saw the angels of retribution, and heard their voices.'

'So in this case it was a motive of revenge, sir?'

'Retribution – not revenge.' Rose appeared to settle down. He put his hands into the pockets of his jacket, pulling the garment tightly about his hips and waist. 'Perfectly justifiable,' he said. And then he inquired: 'D'you understand the meaning of retribution, as distinct from that of revenge, Inspector?'

Collings wasn't entirely certain that he did, and remained silent, going through a notation motion again.

'You don't, do you? I thought not. Then I'll tell you,' Rose said quickly, glancing in Baker's direction with a sneer. 'The word retribution means a recompense for evil acts, against a person – a person like me . . . me, who never had a chance to attain field rank like so many of my business associates and friends. It wasn't my fault that I didn't. D'you understand? Do you?'

'And the word revenge, sir?' Collins asked woodenly.

'Revenge means a vindictive desire to destroy. A *vindic-*

tive desire, Collins. I am not a vindictive man. I am a just man, and an honest and sincere man.'

'And had you made field rank there would have been no cause . . .'

'I'm trying to tell you that, aren't I?' Rose shouted back. 'I know of what I'm capable. I could have been . . .' he suddenly slumped into one of the delicate antique chairs beside him, hands still in pockets, head forward, staring down at the thick carpet.

'I don't think we need trouble you any longer, sir,' Collins eventually muttered, jerking his head at Baker. 'We may have reason to come back and see you . . .'

'I always live here,' Rose said to the floor. 'This is my house. I own this house. Are you going to charge me – you must caution me first, you know.'

'Not at the moment, Mr. Rose. You've been very helpful.'

When they were going down the stairway to the ground floor, Baker asked: 'D'you reckon he's paranoid, sir?'

'I just wouldn't know, Bill. Tell you this though, we're going to have the sub-aqua team in the river at North Bridge as soon as daylight comes in tomorrow. Without that Nambu, we haven't a single hope.'

'It might be in the house.'

'Rose may be odd, but he isn't that crazy. If the team find the Nambu in the river, then we'll know just how odd he is.'

Collins was moving his mental gear shift into a different notch, going back in time and making comparisons with a strangely similar case in the files. Pausing before they got into the patrol car between the big Bentley and the vintage Lea Francis, he asked Baker: 'Remember the Peter Manuel case, Bill?'

'Too well,' Baker replied. 'More than well. Jack Lodge ran a feature on the Manuel shootings in his paper a week ago.'

Collins stopped for thought. Then he said to the driver: 'Drive us down to the *Courier* office, and snap it up.'

12

They compared the brisky terse prose of the newspaper feature with the notes collected regarding the suspect James Craig Rose. There was a highly informative file on the Manuel shootings available at Central, but Collins was impatient to a degree of annoyance now. From the direction of the charge room they were aware of high-pitched protestations being emitted by a couple of drunken tinkers who had been picked up, neck full of raw spirits and wine, trying to knock each other's head off in a public convenience. Awaiting interrogation elsewhere in the building were two thieves, a prostitute, a shoplifter and an aged male whose pride in his sexual organs was such that he was in the habit of displaying them to children in alleys. All part of the daily rubbish of life.

Collins and Baker stood side by side and carefully read the small paragraphs. A two-and-a-half inch print of Peter Manuel graced the edge of the feature directly underneath the headline. Jack Lodge, who as a reporter at the time, had covered the case in the High Court fifteen years earlier, and was now reviewing the facts.

Manuel had taken two detectives to the river where he had pointed to a spot and had told them that one of his guns had been dropped in there.

Collins said: 'Rose maintains he dropped the Nambu into the river at North Bridge.'

Manuel was ambitious and above all else had a vivid imagination with dreams of grandeur in which he was a clever, resourceful person.

'That might fit Rose, too, sir,' Baker observed thoughtfully.

'Rose wanted above all else to attain field rank,' Collins said, 'so as to be equal to some of his friends and business associates. He has his Bentley and his Audi cars, his expensive flat, money, and whatever . . . but can't call himself colonel or even major.' The telephone diverted their attention. Collins picked it up and said: 'Inspector Collins.'

'The medical examiner's here, sir. Will I bring him in?' Steve Pearson's voice answered.

'Thank you, Steve. Do that please.' He replaced the phone and read another paragraph. 'You know this, Bill? I'm nearly ready to bet you even money that Rose read this feature last week. The one way we can gain access to that official medical history is to book him, hold him and then get the P.F. organized on securing it.'

'Morning, lads.' The time was on the minute of eighteen hundred hours, but Jock Cameron seldom observed such niceties. 'How's the man, Jumbo?'

'About ready to cry my eyes out, Doc,' Collins said glumly, his eyes on the newspaper on his desk. 'We're having a squint at the Manuel case. Mind if I pick your brains for a minute, Doc, regarding paranoia? A hypothetical case, of course.'

'Oh, of course; a hypothetical case. That's all right.' Cameron smiled and placed a cigarette dead in the centre of his mouth and lit it delicately. Then he smiled through the smoke, thinly, signalling that he was on the appropriate wavelength, as the burly inspector liked to quote from time to time.

Collins was exploring the cavity between his teeth with his tongue as he considered how to open the inquiry. 'What causes it; in the first place, I mean?'

'I'm no psychiatrist, Jumbo.'

'You know how I occasionally feel about head-shrinkers, Doc.'

'They have their uses, really.'

'Ah,' Collins uttered sourly, and waited.

'Well, let's see,' Cameron began slowly. 'Paranoia might be described, up to a point, as a mental disease that affords the patient certain delusions of grandoise existence; living in a dream world, if you like.'

'Like the famous Walter Mitty, for example,' Baker suggested.

'In a way. Over estimation of self. Expansive quite often. Rather too well dressed for their position in life . . .' Cameron paused. 'Is this helping you?'

'It's helping, Doc,' Collins said, nodding. 'When does it begin? From injury to the brain . . . is one born with it . . . does it happen suddenly?'

'I suppose we're all a bit paranoid from time to time.' Cameron smiled again. 'Like me, when I tell myself I'm nearly as good as Lee Trevino, but I don't have his incredible luck with chip shots to the green. I suppose a brain injury could bring it to light – make it more pronounced, that is. But I don't really know for certain. I'm a simple, wee butcher boy, as you know.'

'Such modesty, Doc,' Collins said sadly. 'Would the client be a clever laddie? By which question I mean – would he have the will, the determination, the planning skill to carry out a sophisticated murder, or execution, if you prefer?'

Cameron considered that for some time. Then he answered: 'From past examinations and the like in which I've been directly involved, I'd offer the theory that a fair amount of unsolved killings have been committed by paranoids; if only because of the fact that no feasible motive was established. You see, this is the important point, so long as such a person believes, sincerely believes in what he is doing, or is about to do, he'll do it very well. Review your case there in the newspaper. According to Manuel's confession he had shot his first victim more than two years – two *years* – before he was arrested. I'd classify that as being done very well . . . if you understand what I'm trying to say.'

'I get you,' Collins agreed. 'So our hypothetical client has the thinking still . . . okay. The determination?'

'I'd say yes.'

'A big grudge lasting a long period of time against his victim?'

'Now that, I'm not certain about. Possibly, yes. It might escalate over the years, with the paranoia becoming progressive.'

'How about trying to tell police officers a batch of ghost stories; big, fancy ghosters?'

'He might do that rather well, too . . . for a while.'

'For a while,' Collins repeated; 'how long a while?'

'Under interrogation – might last half an hour, possibly more than that – then he'd probably crumple and become quite inconsistent.'

Collins caught Baker's eye and the stare was returned. Baker then glanced at the notes available. Eventually he nodded. Baker asked quietly: 'Would our client go to all this rigmarole of confession and so on, even if he hadn't been anywhere near the locus at the moment in time?'

'He might well do. Again, I repeat, I'm not an expert in this particular field. The degree of eccentricity can become quite bizarre – quite incredibly . . . well, incredible, if you like.'

'But cunning with it,' Collins suggested.

Cameron shrugged. 'Maybe, Jumbo.'

'Ah,' Collins said briefly.

Cameron scratched the heavily freckled back of his right hand and asked: 'Do *you* believe that our . . . hypothetical suspect . . . did the shooting of our . . . hypothetical victim, Jumbo?'

'I don't know, Doc,' Collins eventually admitted. 'I quite honestly don't know. What's so much more important, with what evidence I have, I couldn't prove it.'

'How about you, Bill?' Cameron asked.

'I'm just a simple wee copper, Doc.'

'Aren't we all?' Collins muttered.

At first light the following morning, the sub-aqua team went into action. Dick Rimmer drove a plain brown van down a paved ramp that led under the arch of North Bridge. The van bore the insignia of the Department of the Environment, and Rimmer wore a cloth cap and an overall suit of workmen's dungarees. He was aware of a sour odour as he clambered out of the cab. The archway was regularly used for the purpose of drinking methylated spirits, injecting drugs into already shattered bloodstreams, manufacturing unwanted children, the temporary usage of prostitutes, and a recognized vomiting venue for weekend drunks. On the adjacent concrete wall various and several latter day Plutarchs had expelled their obscene literary frustrations with the aid of aerosol paint sprays. Rimmer read them carefully, silently deploring the standard of spelling, while the three-man team of police frogmen adjusted their bottles and ballast belts.

Unknown to any of the four operators, they were being observed through binoculars from the window of a director's office on the eighth floor of a high-rise office block.

Rimmer lit his second cigarette of the day and spat into the grey river water, momentarily happy with the thought that his was not the uneviable task of his companions. He watched them slipping into the river in silence and then went back to peruse the uplifting information offered by the second edition of the national daily paper.

Reading, he waited patiently.

Watching, the observer in the office also waited patiently.

At that same moment in time, fifty one miles north of the river, Hamish MacInnes crawled out of his bivouac tent and, under the rain slicker about his shoulders, ruefully urinated on the wet grass of the small meadow behind the Spruces.

167

His initial task had been to establish the presence of Joy Sinclair in the district, on or about the premises, and the relevant date or dates thereof. Upon ringing in his initial report the previous evening, he had been instructed to stay with it until further orders.

He had stayed with it. He had failed to discover even a word of relevant information appertaining to the inquiry. From nine-thirty until midnight he had been required to make himself pleasant at the bridge table where, much to his disgust, his hosts had repeatedly devastated his game, apologizing kindly in the process. Worse still, they had proved to be total abstainers, and the complete and utter absence of an encouraging dram had reduced him to a quivering dreg. The final indignity had appeared an hour before the dreary dawn, when a chestnut pony had entered the meadow. The animal, possibly spooked by the presence of strange smells and flapping canvas, had chosen to vent its fear or annoyance by kicking over the end pole before emitting a whinny of alarm and fleeing the meadow, leaving the camper calling down the wrath of God and doing his hopeless best to readjust himself to his surroundings.

MacInnes therefore took the law into his own hands, packing up his belongings, stowing them in the boot of his VW, and vowing that it was time he threw his warrant in Frank Wishart's face, and quite prepared to accord the North Division Superintendent three hearty cheers while so' doing. He drove the VW out of the meadow, down the main drive to the road and headed for the nearest telephone kiosk.

At eight-fifteen, he rang in to report.

Charger Steed's raucous tones replied: 'You've got to come in. Where have you been all night?'

'On my annual holidays, Sergeant,' MacInnes answered wearily. 'I'll be so glad when they've over. Really I will, right enough.'

'You trying to come the tin man with me, Mac?' Steed demanded.

'Don't be unkind, Sarge . . . else I'm going to burst into tears.'

MacInnes hung up and left the kiosk. He was beginning to shiver slightly, and he had the impression that his feet would never ever regain their normal temperature. A dram – or five drams – might do something for the sluggish nature of his bloodstream. And old MacLean the chemist might be up and about; for it had never been known for a South Uist man to refuse another a glass of medication at a time like this.

Hamish MacInnes sneezed violently, shivered involuntarily again, endeavoured to cheer his suffering soul with the thought of a tumbler of toddy in the old chemist's kitchen, and drove the VW in that direction.

Only to be informed upon arrival at the MacLean establishment that the proprietor, a decent citizen brought up in the true faith of his native island, had gone to morning Mass at the chapel.

With despair in his heart, and fleeting thoughts of arsenic or something worse in his mind, Hamish MacInnes drove back to North Division, sneezing repeatedly.

Back under the arch of North Bridge, Dick Rimmer watched the head and shoulders of the first of the frogmen emerging from the grey river. The frogman carried a plastic sack strapped about his waist, as did his companions. As Rimmer was about to ask what progress he had made, the frogman shook his head and removed his mask.

The second diver emerged and unstrapped his sack and tossed it to the waiting man. Rimmer felt the sack with his finger tips and smiled; sourly, but with a sense of hope. They had found the gun.

The third diver eventually climbed on to the ramp and his head nodded before his mask came off. Rimmer took the sack from him and examined its contents.

They had found two guns on the riverbed.

The observer in the office block watched the weapons being examined through ten-power lenses. As the van drove away, he threw back his head and laughed, for quite a long time. James Craig Rose was evidently very amused indeed.

By the time Collins appeared at North Division, Steve Pearson had come on duty in the charge room. Two uniformed policewomen were escorting a trio of female teen-agers to one of the waiting rooms. Collins scanned the faces of the trio and raised one eyebrow at the duty sergeant.

'Jumped the wall at approved school last night. We picked them up at the railway station. Someone's coming up with a social worker to handle it.' Pearson dismissed the unimportant matter by presenting a flimsy to the inspector. 'Old Guido Bolesco died at half four,' he said. 'Father Cabrelli rang in asking did we want him for anything.'

Collins shook his head, reading the flimsy. Chick Harmon in the special ward wanted to talk to him as soon as possible. 'Get the exchange on to Pete Culbard, Steve. I'll take it in my office.'

'Aye, right away, Jumbo. Having any luck yet?'

Collins shook his head silently, about to turn away towards the corridor. 'Chick Harmon's about our only hope, I'd say.'

'The sub-aqua boys turned in a gun; two guns, in fact. I put the report on your desk.' The sergeant grinned. 'How about that?'

Collins moved out of the charge room quickly. He had to make an appearance in court at noon to give evidence. That gave him – and he checked his watch – two and a half hours to sew up the Bolesco execution. He felt almost cheerful when Bill Baker stood up as he entered his office. 'Morning Bill. How's the boy?'

'Not so bad, sir. We got the gun.'

'I heard. Where is it? Forensic?'

Baker nodded, picking up the telephone and asking for that department. Twenty seconds passed and he handed the instrument over.

Collins said: 'Inspector Collins. Can I speak to Sergeant Main?'

'Speaking, sir.'

'What's the griff on the weapon you have?'

'Serial number filed out, sir. Two shots fired, but cases still in the cylinder and if you can let me have . . .'

'In the cylinder, you said? A revolver?'

Main confirmed, and added: 'Three-eight calibre, British Enfield Number Two, Mark One. It's the model issued to Army officers at the outbreak and immediately before the outbreak of World War Two. The early model that only functions in double action. You cannot cock it by thumbing the hammer back. I'm going to try the indentation . . .'

'I know the model, George. I understand two guns were retrieved from the river at North Bridge. What's the second one like?' Collins asked. 'Are we on to this Nambu?'

'No, sir. The second gun's a kid's cap pistol, modelled on the old fashioned Wild West six-shooter type. The hammer's been broken off – dumped by some youngster, I'd reckon.'

Collins sighed audibly. 'Okay; thanks, George.'

'I'll try the indentation test and see if we can get a lead on the serial number beneath the filing.'

'Suit yourself. I think I know who that revolver belonged to, George. But it isn't the one that killed Tony Bolesco. We're still looking for that seven mil Nambu.'

'Yes, sir.'

'That's all meanwhile.' Collins replaced the telephone. To Baker, he muttered: 'I'll bet my last oncer that's Rose's service pistol. He really did dump it in the river, like he said.'

'We still have the search warrant, sir.'

'If we go over his drum in King Harald Street, and we find the Nambu in there, I'll sign over my pension to you.'

The telephone interrupted them. Baker said: 'C.I.D. D.C. Baker. Oh, hello; yes, he's right here. Sergeant Culbard, sir, from the special ward.'

Taking the instrument, Collins said: 'Morning, Pete, what's on with the Harmon comedian?'

'Wants to talk to you personally, Jumbo,' the ward orderly said. 'I can plug in a phone at his bedside . . . if you . . .'

'Put him on, Pete.'

Presently Harmon's voice said: 'That you, Jumbo?'

'I have that pleasure, Chick. How you feeling today?'

'I've got a right sore head, so I have.'

'What comes of having nothing inside it, boy.'

'Hey, when you letting me out of here? You'n me made a bargain.'

'It's still on. You know the terms.'

'That's what I want to speak to you . . .'

'Go ahead; speak up. I'm getting deaf in my old age.' Collins said wearily. 'What's on then?'

'I remember what I couldn't remember yesterday. You going to let me out of here? The quack says I'm doing all right now.'

'Let's hear you first, Chick.'

'It was his hands, see?'

Collins said: 'Aye, I see fine. His hands – they were all scarred down the backs. Right?'

'Hey, how'd you know about that?' Harmon stuttered out.

'I'm a mind reader, Chick. Didn't you know that?'

'Hey, wait a minute – how about me getting out of . . .'

But Collins had slammed the receiver back in its bracket.

Baker glanced at his superior and busied himself with unnecessary concentration on a page of scribbled shorthand notes, waiting to take an order, waiting to offer a suggestion if his mind felt up to it and hoping it might be of some use.

Collins unfolded his mind and proceeded to recapitulate. He had been concerned, directly and indirectly, with nineteen clients during the Bolesco inquiry. He could remember them all clearly. Chick Harmon; the two truck drivers who had seen something of the incident; the editor Jack Lodge;

172

the four nuts – Benjie Booth, Gregory Hamilton, Torquil Ossian MacKaskill, James Craig Rose; Robert Tullo Whitehead and Harold Potter; Albert Younger; the waitress Maisie; Nat MacDowell; Joy Sinclair; Irish Pat; Nel Abney; Derek Spenser Quigley; Guido Bolesco, and Father Mario Cabrelli.

Villiers, Duffy and Kruse were the dead: they would stay dead. They were so much better dead.

Who had shot Big Tony? Nel Abney? Irish Pat? Fat Nat? James Craig Rose; Or, possibly, Joy Sinclair?

Collins thought about the woman again: she had always been a possibility, though very much at the back of his mind. If, as now seemed likely, she and Rose had been having it off nicely at the Spruces and elsewhere, the Sinclair bird had a motive. Had Big Tony confided the location of his loot before being picked up? If so, all the more reason for la Sinclair to carry out the shooting. With the cooperation of James Craig Rose?

Collins cancelled Irish Pat, Fat Nat from the short list. Nel Abney would be, was being, checked out already. Abney was a foreigner in the manor: he had never been known as a member of the Bolesco mob, or as a member of any of the city mobs. Albert Younger? Collins cancelled Albert Younger immediately.

Nel Abney or James Craig Rose. Or Joy Sinclair.

'Bill,' he said thoughtfully, 'I have to be in court shortly. Take Dick Rimmer and present our mutual compliments to Joy Sinclair. Give her some treatment. Let her know – you know the form – that we are aware of her association with Rose. Put on all the pressure you like. If she proves to be awkward or smart, whip her up here and hold her on suspicion. I'll deal with her myself if necessary.' Collins let his tongue explore the gap in his teeth. 'And look in on Pete Culbard at the special ward: he can knock off as from now, and the duty man as well. Harmon's free to leave if the M.O. approves his fitness.'

'Yes, sir.' Baker waited on expectantly.

'What is it, Bill?' Collins eventually asked him.

'I was thinking about the search warrant, sir; for King Harald Street.'

Collins produced the warrant and passed it across his desk. 'If you must. What I said about my pension still holds. If you do decide to go through that drum, though I'm convinced you're going to be wasting your time, you can mention to Rose that we'd like to come along and identify his service revolver.'

Baker's face betrayed slight astonishment. 'Very well, sir,' he agreed dubiously.

'Might be interesting. Bill. Again, it mightn't.'

'Did Rose shoot Bolesco, sir?'

Collins nodded. 'Aye, Rose shot Tony Bolesco, Bill. With a gun we cannot find, and never will find, unless by some miracle. And the miracles never come into this office.'

'We might persuade him to tell us where the gun is, sir,' Baker suggested.

Collins smiled thinly, almost sneered. 'We'd have to call him major or colonel in order to do that, Bill. Can you see the picture, eh? We nick him and give him some interrogation treatment; a client who's been through it all before, only ten times, a hundred times, worse than anything we can throw at him. We aren't allowed to use red hot bayonets, either. Rose brings in his mouthpiece, and his personal head shrinker, and both those funny little men make a point of broadcasting the injustice of the police. The brutal treatment of a sick man, an unsung hero of the jungles. And what would we get at the end of the day? A jumble of inconsistent nonsense.'

Baker could see the point. Juries had to have evidence; not inconsistent nonsense. 'Yes, sir. I'll get Rimmer now.' The young detective put the search warrant into his pocket, and asked hesitantly: 'Is there . . . anything further you'd . . .'

'No, Bill, I don't think there's anything else for the moment.'

'Very well, sir.'

The time was ten-thirty a.m. as Baker left the office.

Collins remained seated at his desk. He sat there for quite a long time.

When Steve Pearson knocked and entered the office at eleven-thirty, Collins was still seated at his desk. For the space of one hour in time he had thought, reflected, theorized, concentrated, bringing out names and faces, remembering form sheets, going over the multitude of clients who had had connections with the Bolesco mob in the past; and the more he had concentrated, the more convinced he had become that James Craig Rose had executed Tony Bolesco.

With one or two classical exceptional examples, serious crime took on a shape, form, a system. The forensic boys knew their stuff. Collins reckoned he knew his stuff, too. As did Bill Baker, Rimmer, and the other members of the team – the teams – all over the country. They all knew, on a job, who had committed the crime; but then came the crunch of solving it, conclusively, and submitting the necessary evidence in a court-room that would convince a jury, despite the orations and protestations of the mouthpieces, and the head shrinkers. One of a kind of same was enough for any simple policeman; but when they joined forces and teamed up to fight the righteous battle for the defence of the poor, much maligned, helpless, irresponsible, sick, pathetic accused . . . that was where the opposition got too stiff.

That was when the policeman had to bow out, respectably, regretfully, yet grudgingly, and naturally so, to forces far above his station. Juries had to have irrefutable evidence. Collins looked up as the duty sergeant entered the office.

'Yes, Steve, what is it now?'

'I . . . em, just looked in to remind you there's that court on at twelve, Jumbo.'

'Ah. Aye, thanks, Steve. I was going a wee bit of thinking.'

'Aye, about – oh, aye. Anything coming through?'

'I've almost as much hope,' Collins admitted slowly, 'of solving Big Tony's murder . . . as, as I have of finding holy water in hell.'

Collins got up, put on his coat and hat and walked out of the office.

Outside on the street, the rain belted down upon the paving slabs. A murky thickness in the air presaged another mist about to come up from the river.

Collins pulled up the collar of his coat, and trudged down to the courthouse in the rain.

13

They found Joy Sinclair in one of the two offices behind the Crystal Club. She evinced no visible surprise at their arrival and, after waving a pen in the direction of two available chairs, went on with the bookwork on the table before her. She was thus engaged when Fat Nat MacDowell appeared with a bottle and four glasses. Dick Rimmer glanced at the bottle, scowled, and unwrapped a stick of spearmint gum and folded it into his mouth. Baker didn't speak. Joy Sinclair looked up and returned her attention to the columns of her accounts. Fat Nat was in the process of pouring an ample measure of Scotch into the third glass when the first word was uttered.

Rimmer said: 'Not for us, Nat. Too early in the day. It's just after twelve noon.'

Fat Nat's chins quivered with silent mirth. 'You know what they say in the Navy about the sun being . . .'

'We know what they say in the Navy,' Baker said evenly.

'What's the matter, lads?'

'We're working,' Rimmer explained sourly. 'We want to have a pleasant, private little chat with Joy here. I repeat – private.'

'What about?' the woman demanded without looking up.

'We can proceed with the chat at North Division if you like,' Rimmer suggested. 'It's raining cats and dogs outside, and we'll all be walking. Suit yourself, Joy.'

'Very well,' she agreed. 'I'll have that one, Nat.' She took one of the glasses, topped it up with the extra Scotch from the third one, and disposed of about half of the Scotch in a slow swallow. 'And now? How may I be of assistance to you, gentlemen?'

'If Nat will kindly blow, we'll tell you,' Baker informed her.

'Blow, Nat.'

After five seconds of hesitation, Nat blew.

Joy Sinclair said: 'Cheers,' and finished the Scotch.

Rimmer pressed the partially masticated gum against his front teeth with the ball of his thumb, and said: 'Strath Garry. We're looking into a job up there. In the course of investigation, your name turned up. So that's why we're here. Okay?'

'My name turned up?' She expressed open astonishment, false or otherwise. It didn't matter.

'When you signed yourself as Miss or Mrs. Rose – or Ross – in the poison register of the local chemist. Remember him – the chemist? Mr. MacLean, M.P.S. When your bronchitis was giving you gipp.'

'That was ages ago,' she admitted.

'December twenty-third, 1971, to be absolutely exact,' Baker said.

'Where were you living at the time?' Rimmer interrupted.

'I was . . . doing a cabaret at a house party. It was Christmas time. I was afraid of losing my voice and went . . .'

'Yes, we know all about that, Joy,' Rimmer told her sourly. 'But where? Whose house party?'

'A friend of mine.'

'Name of friend of yours?'

'Jimmy Rose.'

'So you uttered a false name for the purpose of . . .'

'. . . obtaining a few ephedrine tablets? Oh, come off it. Haven't you pretty men more to do than . . .'

'Tell us about Jimmy Rose, Joy,' Baker said.

'He used to come here to the club. He asked me if I'd like to do a song and dance turn at his house over the festive season. It was all perfectly above board, I assure you. I lived at the house with the other guests. Anyway, what's Jimmy done?'

'Nothing that we can prove,' Baker said, smiling at the woman. 'What else went on at the house party?'

'The usual sort of thing – there was a band; piano, guitar and bass. Lots of food and nice things to drink. The men went shooting and we women sat around and gossiped about this and that.'

'Shooting what?' Rimmer demanded.

'How'd you mean?' Joy Sinclair eventually asked them.

'What did they shoot – or shoot at . . . grouse, pheasants, hares or what?' Baker was quick to note the woman's caution.

She said: 'They used to shoot in the orchard. At those saucer things – skeet pigeons, or something. Jimmy wasn't very good at it . . .'

'Go on, my little flower,' Rimmer purred at her.

'It's about the accident with the pistol you came about, isn't it?' She began to reach for the glass but, finding it empty, she lit a cigarette from a silver box beside her on the table. They watched the nervous flicker of the lighter's flame.

'Tell us about the accident with the pistol, Joy,' Baker said.

'One of the guests got shot in the leg by mistake. Jimmy wasn't very good at shooting the skeet pigeons, so he challenged some of the others to shoot at the paper targets he had pinned up to a frame. He was very good at pistol shooting. And . . . someone let off the pistol and someone else got hit in the leg. God's truth – after all this time.'

'Who got shot? Who fired the shot?' Baker asked her.

'It was a man called Campbell; Adam Campbell, I think. But he was all right. The bullet went right through. Someone treated him – someone in the party. It was all hushed up.'

'Mixing booze with gunpowder, was it?' Rimmer asked.

'Might have been. I wasn't there, in the orchard, I mean. I

only got to know about it when I got back to the house, in the evening. I'd gone for a walk to the village . . . or somewhere.'

'You're doing very well,' Baker said pleasantly. 'Tell us about the range in the orchard, where the targets were pinned up.'

So Joy Sinclair, unaware of the real purpose of their visit, told them about the range in the orchard.

By two-forty-five that same afternoon, Rimmer and Baker were presenting themselves to the tall woman who lived at the Spruces near the village of Strath Garry.

Sergeant Steve Pearson and Inspector Jumbo Collins came out of the courthouse, automatically turning up their coat collars against the persistent rain, and walked back to North Division. They had been stuck in a witness room for precisely three hours before the court usher had called Collins to the box. There, he had given evidence for over forty minutes before being instructed to stand down. Steve Pearson had followed and had delivered his share of the evidence for fifteen minutes. The case was that of car theft followed by a break-in. The offence had taken place six weeks earlier. The hearing continued.

They hardly exchanged a word until they reached North Division at four-fifty-five that afternoon. In the locker room they hung up their coats and placed chilled hands on the steam-heated radiator, each mentally reviewing the prospects of the hearing and each doubtful about its successful outcome. The client involved had a form sheet like a Derby winner; but it could go either way, for all that.

'Let's try the canteen for a start, Steve,' Collins suggested.

'Aye, Jumbo, that's a fair plan. I could do fine with a gargle of something a bit stronger than coffee, though; much stronger.'

'Me, too,' Collins agreed glumly, and led the way down the green walled corridor, navigating accurately by the aroma of hot sausage rolls and other delicacies from their destination.

They were still there when Dick Rimmer entered and glanced round the collection of officers and policewomen at the tables and at the counter. High on a television shelf in a corner niche of the wall, a BBC news-reader was announcing the details of an attempt to hold up a Royal limousine in, of all thoroughfares, the Mall in London. The episode had happened the previous evening. Now came the details of the Bow Street preliminaries. The world had become so crazy that anything could happen; even green snow on the Cairngorm ski-slopes.

Rimmer spared about fifteen seconds to direct a soured glance at the television set, his jaws working on spearmint gum, and then he moved across to the counter where Collins and Pearson were in the process of demolishing their third sausage roll and second cup of coffee in morose silence, apparently utterly unmoved by the stirring news from the box.

'Excuse me, sir,' Rimmer said quietly.

'We struck at the Crystal Club; with la Sinclair, sir.'

Collins swallowed the remaining wad of sausage roll in a gulp, and said: 'Ah.' Then he finished the coffee in the cup, eructated gently, and wiped morsels of flaky pastry off his hands. 'So?'

'Bill and I went up to Strath Garry,' Rimmer explained, and held out his right hand, palm upward. In the palm lay a copper-jacketed lead bullet, the metal casing slightly green due to oxidization. 'We found twenty-one others like it . . . in a sandbank in the wifie's orchard.'

'So?' Collins said blankly, examining the missile. Despite the oxide on the copper jacket, traces of rifling were evident to the naked eye.

'We've got the others on your desk.'

'We'd better have a look at the others,' Collins said. 'Coming, Steve?'

'Aye, sure.'

In his office, Collins examined the productions with great

care. A number of them had been carefully cleaned of all green oxide. Several of the expended bullets had been deformed by impact against stone or possibly metal. The majority, except for very minor scratches, were more or less in their original shape. Those that had been cleaned were encased in strong celophane envelopes, labelled and signed by Rimmer and Bill Baker; the labels also bore the time, date and location where the missiles had been recovered. On the underside of the labels, Collins recognized the initials of Sergeant George Main of Forensic.

He said: 'Ah.'

'Seven millimetre calibre, sir.'

'Nambu?' Collins asked.

'We've got a trio of clients who were at the booze-up at the time. Picked them up on the way in, about half an hour ago. They're in Number Three waiting-room, waiting to tell you about the Nambu.'

Collins expressed momentary ignorance of the situation, and Rimmer recounted the interview with la Sinclair, and what had followed. Steve Pearson's face began to soften into something approaching a beatification.

'What a clever little lad you've turned out to be, Dickie,' he said.

'Thank you, Sergeant,' Rimmer answered woodenly.

Collins allowed his face to go lopsided as his tongue found the cavity between his teeth. 'Do they match the rounds Doc Cameron hacked out of Tony Belesco?'

Bill Baker tendered a sheet of hastily typed foolscap. 'This is the initial report from Sergeant Main, sir. We asked him to give it priority, in this instance.'

Collins read the typed statement. Then he said to Steve Pearson: 'Organize a warrant for the arrest of James Craig Rose, Steve, if you please.'

'Aye, sure, right away, sir.' Pearson left the office.

'Will there be enough to work on, sir?' Baker asked quietly.

'That, Bill, will be for the Procurator Fiscal to decide. Far's I'm concerned, we might just manage with what we've got.' Collins turned to Dick Rimmer, and asked : 'You think so, Dick?'

'Search me, sir,' Rimmer answered sourly, yet smiling thinly as he chewed on the spearmint gum. 'Imagine — evidence like this turning up after three years.'

'Happened before,' Collins reminded him.

'Let's hope it'll continue that way,' Rimmer said sourly.

'Go out and bring him in, lads,' Collins instructed. He consulted his wrist watch. It was almost six p.m. 'When you book him and tuck him up downstairs, come back here . . . I might even manage to buy you a couple of pints.'

Rather irreverently, Rimmer breathed : 'Wonders will never cease.'

And they went out to bring in James Craig Rose.

As they got into the patrol car in the yard, Baker suddenly exclaimed : 'It's stopped raining, Dick.'

'Aye, so I noticed, Bill. Let's go.'